The Hollow Tree

LOWE[R]
CANA[DA]
(QUEBE[C])

UPPER
CANA[DA]
(ONTARI[O])

ST. LAWRENCE RIV[ER]

ROUTES
→ PHOEBE'S TREK
⬝⬝⬝⬝⬝⬝ JEM'S TREK
+++++++ ROBINSON'S TREK
⋯⋯⋯⋯ REFUGEE'S TREK
–––––– THE MILITARY ROAD
MEETING LOCATIONS
① PHOEBE MEETS PETER SAUK
② START OF JEM'S JOURNEY
③ ROBINSONS AND VERMONT
   LOYALISTS MEET
④ PHOEBE AND JEM MEET
⑤ PHOEBE AND JEM MEET
   OTHER REFUGEES
⑥ PHOEBE CUTS JAPHET ORAM
   FREE AND RUNS OFF
⑦ PHOEBE AND JEM SAY
   GOODBYE

HAWTHORNE BAY

LAKE ONTARIO

N
W   E
S

0   50   100

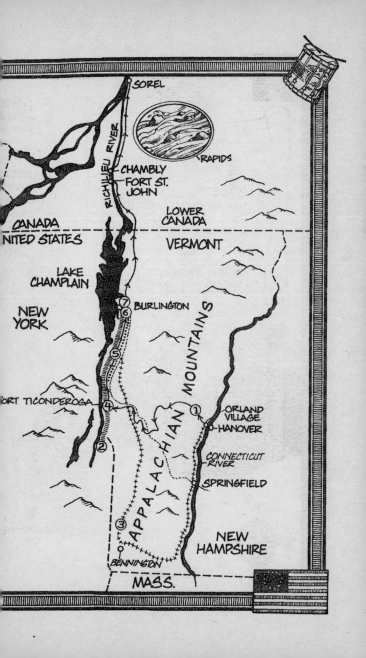

The Hollow Tree

Janet Lunn

Seal Books

Seal Books and colophon are trademarks of Random
House of Canada Limited.

THE HOLLOW TREE
Seal Books/published by arrangement
with Alfred A. Knopf Canada
Alfred A. Knopf Canada edition published 1997
Seal Books edition published August 2001
Cover illustration by Scott Cameron
Page design by Sharon Foster Design
Map by Paul McCusker

ISBN 0-7704-2887-8

Seal Books are published by
Random House of Canada Limited.
"Seal Books" and the portrayal of a seal are the
property of Random House of Canada Limited.

Visit Random House of Canada Limited's website:
www.randomhouse.ca

PRINTED AND BOUND IN THE USA

OPM   10   9   8   7   6   5   4   3   2   1

*For Louise, who understands story
better than anyone else I know, with love
and gratitude.*

*The author wishes to acknowledge the
pre-Harris government Ontario Arts Council,
the Vermont Historical Society, The University
of Vermont Library, the Norwich, Vermont Town
Library, the Trenton, Ontario Public Library,
Angela Thorpe in the Newport, New Hampshire
Public Library, Christopher Marshall, Greg Brant,
John Lunn, the editorial staff at Knopf Canada,
the children at C. M. L. Snider Public School,
Wellington, Ontario, who listened to me read,
and, most of all, Kathryn McCarthy for her
patience and good humour through countless
reworkings of this manuscript.*

CHAPTER 1

By the River

Throughout all her long life, Phoebe Olcott never forgot a single moment of the last happy afternoon she spent at home by the Connecticut River. It was on a day in May, in the year 1775, and she spent it in her favourite spot on the river bank on the Vermont side.

Phoebe lived with her father in the little wilderness settlement of Hanover, on the New Hampshire side of the wide river. Five years earlier, their ox carts piled high with their belongings, the Olcotts had made the long trek north from their settled town in Connecticut when Eleazer Wheelock had moved both his Presbyterian college and the Indian school north to Hanover. Jonathan Olcott had come to teach at the college.

Teachers and students alike had set to, with a will, to fell the enormous white pines and build their habitations, but, in 1775, the college was still only a collection of rough buildings surrounding the stump-filled clearing called The Green. To Phoebe it was the centre of the world and she loved it. She loved the big unpainted dormitories and classrooms and the big college barn at the corner of The Green. She loved Dr. Wheelock's house, which everyone called The Mansion House. She loved the ringing sound of iron on iron that emerged from the fiery depths of Israel Curtis's blacksmith shop as he fashioned horseshoes and door hinges and fire boxes, and she loved Master Seaver's carpentry shop with its scent of fresh pine wood shavings. She even loved Captain Storr's tavern, although she never went there and the laughter and the shouts that erupted from within it sometimes frightened her. She liked the young men better when they came bursting through her own cabin door, drunk on ideas and not on rum.

They came, fired up to argue Greek philosophy and Christian doctrine with Phoebe's father. Sometimes they came with pigeons, partridges, rabbits, or deer slung over their shoulders, ready to butcher for Phoebe to roast over her fire. Phoebe's quiet ways were popular with them. They called her pet names like Mouse, the name her cousin Gideon had for her, or Little Bird, the name the Mohawk Peter Sauk called her.

Phoebe would squeeze herself between the

log wall and the edge of the big stone fireplace in the front room and listen to the talk with longing. She would have liked to join in, but she was too shy. However, she was not too shy to think about the talk and to wish that women could become students at the college and teach there. One day, she supposed, she would marry one of her father's students. He would become a teacher like her father, and life would go on as it had for as long as she could remember.

Her mother and her infant brother had died of measles when she was four. She could remember nothing at all about her brother. She remembered her mother's smile and her soft, low singing, but there was little time in that backwoods life to long or to grieve.

She had had to begin at age four to care for her father and herself. Now, at thirteen, as well as the book learning she had from her father, she could cook wild animals and plants from the forest, as well as the potatoes, pumpkins, and onions she grew in her tiny garden patch. She could spin the tough-fibred flax and soft wool, then weave them together into the linsey-woolsey cloth out of which she made shirts and breeches for her father and simple gowns for herself. Sometimes she even managed to dye the cloth with red from the wild puccoon or brown from the sumac. As well she had learned to make sure her father had his books under his arm, his comforter around his neck, his hat on his head, and his bit of meat and bread in his coat pocket every morning before he set out across The Green to meet his students.

Phoebe often thought of life in the little settlement surrounded by the endless forest as like being inside her cabin with a storm raging outside. The settlement seemed like a haven against all that wildness.

But on this bright afternoon in May, she was not thinking about any of that. She had turned her back on her housework, and she was refusing to think about the war her father and his students always talked about of late. Thoughts of how her impulsive father might rush off to fight in a war made her feel sick in her stomach. No, she could not think about that. She tucked her shawl into her waistband and, bunching her skirts tightly in her hands, she hurried down the steep Hanover hill to the little cove where Master Starling kept his canoe. In exchange for doing his mending, Master Starling, the old bachelor who worked for the blacksmith, let Phoebe use his canoe. She was too frugal to pay the tuppence for the rope ferry and, besides, she loved to pit the strength of her arms against the river's strong current. Skilfully she paddled across the big dark river to the western shore, to where a brook tumbled into the river beside a small beaver meadow about the size of the Olcotts' tiny cabin, protected from the encroaching forest by five giant willow trees.

The sun was high in a deep blue sky, but the air was chilly. A stiff breeze from the east had made the journey easier for Phoebe but hard going for a flock of geese working their way north. As she neared the shore, a pair of otters dived into the water, alarming a blue jay perched on a low branch of one of the willows. It took off with an indignant screech.

She jumped out of the canoe and pulled it up over the stones onto the grass. She sniffed the May-scented air, the freshness of blue violets and yellow adder's-tongues, the sweetness of the trailing arbutus under the last of the snow in the rock shadows at the edge of the meadow; she listened to the *cheek-cheek* of the spring warbler. Tiny pale-green leaves softened the branches of the willow trees. She croaked back at the baby frogs trying out their high, shrill voices along the muddy river bank, then swiftly stepped across the meadow to the biggest tree. Halfway between the ground and its lowest branch was a deep hollow. It was home to a grey squirrel Phoebe had named Constant, after an incessant talker in Hanover. It was also the place Phoebe and her cousins Anne and Gideon Robinson had, years ago, chosen for their letter-box.

Whenever Phoebe could slip away across the river — if there was no time to climb the hill to

Orland Village, where her cousins lived — she would leave a note in the hollow tree. The note would let them know she had been there, give them news, and tell them when she might come again. They would do the same.

Anne was two years older than Phoebe and she liked to remind her cousin of it. She could be sharp-tongued and had a temper that came and went like a lightning storm in June. Phoebe wasn't always comfortable around her, but she couldn't help but admire Anne's high spirits, her easy manner, and the way she attracted people to her. Gideon was two years older than his sister, as serious as Anne was frivolous. Every moment he could steal from his daily chores he spent in the woods, collecting plants. He had no interest in farming or studying at the college with Phoebe's father; all he wanted to do was to catalogue Vermont's wild plants. Phoebe loved Gideon, his steady nature, his rare smiles, his patience with Billy Wilder, the gentle boy the villagers called simple, who followed him everywhere with slavish devotion.

Phoebe and her cousins had been like sisters and brother almost all their lives. Their mothers had been sisters and their fathers were friends. The Robinsons had chosen to settle on the Vermont side of the river because they had come with friends from Connecticut Province who were settling Orland Village. Phoebe's father chose the New Hampshire side because he had accepted a teaching post at the college. But the families, like the two provinces, were separated only by the wide, swift-flowing Connecticut River, so Phoebe and Anne and Gideon met when they could in their favourite meadow. This time there was a crumpled note from Anne. It read only: "Thursday after dinner." And it was Thursday afternoon after dinner.

Before Phoebe had time to do more than lift her skirt and stuff the note into the pocket she wore on a string around her waist under her gown and sit herself down under the tree, Anne was there beside her.

"So" — she smiled down at her cousin — "you came."

"Yes I did, and my hand is sore from spinning, I worked so swiftly this morning. I was bound I would have at least one portion of this perfect day to do with as I pleased. So here I am, but not because of your note. I've only read it this minute."

"Phoebe." Anne shook her head. "You are so dutiful. Do you never, ever just cast off your work without a thought?"

"No. How could I?"

"Well, we are not the same." Anne tossed her shawl to the ground and dropped down on it. "No," she said with a note of satisfaction in her voice, "not at all the same."

Nor were they — not in looks, not in temperament. To begin with, Anne was not only two years older than Phoebe, she was at least four inches taller. She was graceful and slim, with long hands and feet, and light brown hair — which she preferred to call golden — that curled softly around her pale, oval face. Deep violet eyes tilted up at the corners just enough to make her face interesting. She laughed easily with the young men in the village and always had a quick response to their jokes. She was considered by them all to be the best-looking girl in the village — and by a good many of the girls to be the vainest. She dressed every morning with great care and was always neatly turned out. The gown she wore this afternoon was rose-coloured and there was a bit of lace in its collar. Her shawl had a checked pattern in black and white.

Phoebe, on the other hand, was somewhat awkward and she was timid. She was short and round, and she had a round face. Her dark brown hair was so straight and fine that it was forever coming loose from its braid to fly around her face. Her brown eyes were bright and large, her nose small, her mouth wide — much too wide, Anne often told her, but would sometimes add out of kindness, "But your eyes are fine, Phoebe. I expect they are your finest feature."

"Well, they are not crossed and I can see out

of both of them," Phoebe had responded tartly the first time Anne had said that, but, truly, she didn't spend much time thinking about what she looked like or what she wore. There was no lace on her collar and she had not troubled herself to dye the cloth for her everyday gown. It was the much-washed grey-white colour of old linen and wool. She had determined early on that she was no beauty and did not see much point fretting about it.

"Gershom Lake brought me a gift last night," said Anne. She leaned back against the tree. When Phoebe made no response, she asked, "Don't you wish to know what he gave me?" There was a note of annoyance in her voice.

"Oh, I do indeed."

"It is but a little thing," Anne said carelessly, "a good-luck charm, a heart he fashioned from a broken silver spoon of his mother's."

"Oh, my!" Phoebe took the rough little silver heart Anne held out to her. She wondered what it would be like to have a young man bringing her gifts. "It is fine indeed. Do you mean to have Gershom Lake, then?"

"Oh, mercy, no!" Anne took the heart from Phoebe and began to toss it back and forth between her hands. "But I like well the things he brings me." Her smile was so self-satisfied that Phoebe was shocked into saying, "Anne, how can you be so unkind! You'll be left on the shelf with no husband at all. You ——" She stopped. She had no wish to be the target of Anne's sharp tongue. What's more, she knew, only too well, Anne's opinion of her own chances of finding a husband.

"I'll not mind," Anne said with a sniff. "I do not mean to marry a village boy. I mean to go to Boston or New York, or perhaps even across the sea to London. I certainly do not mean to spend my life working myself to the bone in this backwoods. I mean to be a fine lady and wear silk gowns, and kid slippers with diamond buckles on them. Old Mistress Shipley was a fine lady in Boston before her husband was lost at sea with all his ships ——"

"I know. I know all about Mistress Shipley." Phoebe clapped her hand to her heart. "Mistress Shipley has suffered mightily," she intoned, "the slings and arrows of outrageous fortune."

"Honestly, Phoebe" — Anne rose to her feet — "you needn't make speeches at me out of your father's old books. Mistress Shipley was a fine lady, and it's truly dreadful she must live in that horrid shanty. That lazy Robert might at least build a proper house for his mama." Whatever she was going to say next was interrupted by the sound of someone on the forest path. In a moment a tall, brown-haired boy came hurtling down the hill through the bushes into the meadow.

"There's going to be a war," he announced breathlessly. "I knew, of course, there must be. After those idiotic, hot-headed farmers fired on the British soldiers over in Lexington, in Massachusetts, 'twas certain the King would not permit such outrage."

"You knew, of course, you knew," scoffed Anne. She drew her shawl tightly around her shoulders. "But, Gideon, it's not the King who is starting the war — if there is to be a war; it's those farmers and their Boston friends. I heard Papa say that."

"It does not matter, infant." Gideon stood in the centre of the meadow, his feet apart, his hands behind his back, his head thrown back in excitement. "The King will never let them go free with their rebellious nonsense," he said.

He looks like a preacher, thought Phoebe crossly. She loved Gideon so much she abhorred his smallest flaw. And here he stood sounding pompous in his passion.

"Furthermore," said Gideon, "our king will want to know that not everyone in his fourteen American colonies is disloyal. I shall most assuredly have to enlist in his service."

"Oh, la, Gideon." Anne was amused. "You can't do that. Papa will never allow it. You know he will not."

"I know. I know how he hates fighting." Gideon thrust his hands into the pockets of his breeches. "He will say Jesus himself bade us turn the other cheek. But, Nan, war is different. War is...is..." He began pacing back and forth across the little meadow. His stiff self-importance had disappeared. He spun around to face the girls. "This war is important!" he cried. "We cannot let those no-account rowdies like Hiram Jesse and Elihu Pickens run our lives. Some of those traitors are talking about going off to Boston to fight the British soldiers. We have to stop them!"

"Papa says ——" Phoebe began timidly.

"Your p-papa!" Gideon stuttered in his agitation. "Your papa supports those rebels. Patriots, he calls them. Only last week he was sitting in our parlour, supping our cider, talking of Paul Revere and Samuel Adams, those Boston rabble-rousers, as though they were heroes. Before you know it your father will rush off to fight with those Boston rebels. Patriots! How can they call themselves patriots? They're disloyal. They're traitors! Your father is a traitor!"

Phoebe was horrified. Gideon thought it, too: Papa would go off and fight. Suddenly she was sure that Gideon, too, would fight. He would fight for the King. The two people she loved most in the world would go to war and fight on opposite sides. Dear God, they might end by killing each other.

She could not listen to any more. She grabbed

her shawl from the ground where she'd left it and, without a word, crossed the clearing in a dozen steps, pushed the canoe into the water, and jumped in so fast she nearly tipped it over. Quickly she knelt and began paddling furiously towards the New Hampshire shore. She heard but did not answer Anne and Gideon's surprised shouts. She paddled with all her strength against the strong current and a rising wind, glad of the need for the exertion, and the soreness in her arms.

War. They would go to war. Now she could not keep it out of her mind.

Two evenings ago she had heard her father say to his gathering of students, "This war has been in the making for years." On that evening, talk of philosophy had quickly become talk of the right and wrong of war against King George III.

"It was the perfect gesture the Boston patriots made when they threw those chests of tea into the Boston harbour. The perfect gesture!" Papa had slammed his fist down on the heavy wooden table. "The King should know that we cannot, we will not, tolerate taxes on tea or any other goods. If we may not send our elected representatives to the Parliament in Great Britain that makes decisions about our lives, if we are not to be treated like proper British subjects, then, say I, we will no longer be British subjects."

He had pounded so hard on the table that the dishes had bounced on the dresser across the room.

"If it be necessary," he had finished slowly and unexpectedly softly, "every American who cares for the rights of free men must perforce go to war."

The students had left the Olcott cabin that night without their usual banter and their cheery goodbyes. They had been silent, and their faces had borne withdrawn, thoughtful looks.

Now, only two days later, here was Gideon calling her father a traitor and saying that war had begun already, with fighting in Lexington and Concord, near Boston, only one hundred miles away.

Panting from the strenuous paddling and the hurried climb up the hill from the river, Phoebe pushed open the door of her home to find her father sitting by the fire, bent over his musket. He was cleaning it. He looked up and stared blankly at her, as if he wasn't quite sure who she was. She was used to her father's thoughts being far away. "Papa, what are you doing?" she asked, eyeing the musket uneasily.

"Oh, yes, Phoebe, it's you. I'm glad you've come. Phoebe, we are going to war. We are demanding our rights from that obstinate king over in London."

Phoebe blew back a wisp of hair that had

floated into her eyes. She leaned against the door jamb. Her heart-beat was thundering in her ears. She was very frightened. "Papa, you know how you hate firing a gun. You…you are a teacher."

"Daughter, this is not a time to hold back. We in America have tried again and again and yet again to make the government in London understand that we will not be bullied and taxed and ordered about like children. Even here in Hanover we cannot sell our four-hundred-foot pine trees for lumber! They have to go to the government overseas to make masts for British naval ships so that those same ships can keep us in order. It is wrong. So now we must fight!"

It hadn't been an hour since Phoebe had heard those same ringing tones from her cousin Gideon. She tried to swallow back the fear rising like a slow tide inside her. "Papa," she whispered, "you can't go, you'll be killed."

"I must take that chance, child. Heart and mind I stand with the Virginian Patrick Henry, when he said, 'Give me liberty or give me death'!"

The next morning Phoebe watched her father, three other teachers, a dozen students, and other soldiers-to-be from along the Upper Connecticut River gather on The Green to march off through the forest towards Boston to join the growing rebel army. A month later

Jonathan Olcott was killed at the battle of Bunker's Hill, just outside Boston. The booming of the cannons was so intense that the reverberations were felt in Hanover, one hundred miles away.

CHAPTER 2

Traitors and Spies

Two years later, Phoebe was living with her Robinson relatives in Orland Village. Almost fifteen years old in the fall of 1777, she hadn't grown more than an inch. Round-faced, and still a little plump, she still considered herself to be as plain as pudding — something Anne never tired of telling her.

She had not wanted to leave her own cabin home in Hanover. She had wanted to stay and keep it in good order, in part because it soothed her sorrow to keeps things in order, and in part because leaving meant really accepting that her father was never coming home. Uncle Josiah had come for her. Josiah Robinson was a frail, kind man whom people instinctively wanted to save from worry, and Phoebe was a girl who hated to make trouble for anyone. But she was also stubborn about what mattered greatly to her. She refused to budge. In the end, Gideon had had to fetch her.

Phoebe had never been able to refuse Gideon anything. He would come knocking on her door, followed by Billy Wilder, and they would pour out of their sacks the bits of bark, the leaves, the birds' wings they had found for her to organize and label. She had always willingly sorted out and labelled the plant specimens he collected. She had put up with his irritation when she had done things wrong. She had washed and mended his shirts when he had torn or stained them, so his mother would not know. She had even performed that same service for Billy Wilder.

So, when Gideon had come for her, she had packed her spare shift, her spare skirt and petticoat, her Sunday-best gown (the one she had dyed with sumac), and her mother's old fur-lined, tartan wool cloak; picked up the little orange kitten that had been haunting her doorstep; and gone with him.

Aunt Rachael had welcomed her — and the kitten — as Phoebe had known she would, because Aunt Rachael was, though somewhat reserved, a loving woman. She was also strong and able to take charge of any situation, no matter how difficult, which was good because Uncle Josiah was an ineffectual householder, not capable of much beyond his scholarly work, praying for them all.

It had been Gideon who had put his strong ten-year-old arms to work helping the neighbour men and boys clear land and build their first log cabins, ensuring that they, in turn, would help the Robinsons clear, and build their cabin. Uncle Josiah had a small inheritance, so he could pay for help to build a second, bigger frame house. Now it was done, a house with a big chimney that had fireplaces on both sides to warm the keeping-room and hall on one side, the parlour on the other; a pantry, a kitchen with its own fireplace, and Uncle Josiah's study along the back; and up the steep, winding stairs from the hallway, three bedrooms. Uncle Josiah spent most of his time in his study, labouring over the essays he was writing on the Book of Jeremiah. His mind had closed to the war that had drawn so many village men and boys to fight its battles and had set families in the village against each other.

Aunt Rachael had been glad of Phoebe's help with her housework. Anne and Gideon were the oldest of four living children (three babies had died in infancy). The small boys — Jed, five, and Noah, four — were surely, their mother said, "the trials God forgot to send Job." They ran about, paying no heed to their overworked mother or their soft-spoken father. Their sister Anne seemed never to be around when she was needed to look after them. Phoebe often thought, as she chased after the noisy, quarrelsome boys, that they would both be better off if, just once, their father would take his hand to their bare backsides.

But Josiah Robinson was a man who would countenance no violence in his household or out of it. Phoebe was sure that, were Gideon at home, the boys would not so readily run off into the woods, take off for the brook, or torment their little sister.

Gideon was not at home. He had gone off the year before, in July, a month after his nineteenth birthday, a week after the newly formed Continental Congress of the thirteen rebellious American colonies had officially declared their independence from Great Britain. He had gone to fight for the British, for the cause of loyalty and reason, he said, and neither his father's prayers nor his mother's pleas could keep him home.

On the morning he left, after he had said goodbye to the others, he had asked Anne and Phoebe to meet him in their little meadow by the river. He had stood in the bright sunlight and bowed formally first to one, then to the other. "Ladies," he had said, "you see before you a soldier for the King." He had been dressed in his plain brown homespun breeches, waistcoat, and coat, his brown-and-green-striped stockings, and his stout leather shoes. He had looked strong and handsome, and all Phoebe had thought was that he, too, would soon be dead. She hadn't been able to utter a sound until Gideon had put his arms around her and said, "I'll be safe, Mouse, you'll see. I'll be right as rain when we've licked those rogues. Oh!" He'd gulped and tightened his arms around her. "I didn't mean that your father was a rogue, Phoebe, truly I didn't. I know Uncle Jonathan *believed* what he was fighting for, even though — oh, don't cry, Phoebe, please."

"I can't help it."

"Well, you must. You can. You will. Please, Phoebe, I can't bear to march off and have a red blotchy face to remember you by. And you need to help me. You need to comfort Billy Wilder and look after Polly Grantham and see she doesn't marry one of those blasted rebels while I'm saving the country."

He would have said more, but Anne had interrupted.

"Stop your silly blubbering, Phoebe. Only think how splendid Gideon will be." Her eyes had sparkled with excitement. "I don't care what Papa says, Gideon. You will have a beautiful uniform with a scarlet coat and a sword. Were I a boy, I would march off to war with you. Oh, war is so romantic!"

"A fine soldier you'd be with your simpering, flirting ways," Gideon had scoffed. Phoebe had said nothing. She had thought about Uncle Josiah and Aunt Rachael, about Billy Wilder and Polly Grantham. "The dearest, sweetest girl in all the world," Gideon had said about Polly once when Phoebe was helping sort plant specimens. She had turned from him quickly, not wanting him to see how those words hurt. How could someone be dearer and sweeter to him than she was? Gideon had been dearer to her than her own father. She had never built romantic day-dreams around him as she had around some of her father's students, that wasn't how she loved him, but to hear that someone else was the dearest, sweetest girl in all the world was painful.

But, in this moment of goodbye, she had not even minded about Polly Grantham. All she had thought was that Gideon was going to war, Gideon who studied the forest as diligently as her father had studied his books. He was no more a soldier than her father had been. Why did he care so much for the King that he would leave his precious plants to go off and fight? Why had her father cared so much for being free of that king that he had let himself be killed for it? Wasn't it enough for them that they had a warm house to keep out the rain and snow, a garden patch to grow vegetables in, flax and wool to have cloth from?

There didn't seem to be any answer to these questions. But, there was Gideon, standing with the sun shining on his bare head, his brown hair neatly braided and tied with his best black ribbon in its soldierly queue, his face full of resolve.

Now, more than a year later, as the maple trees turned bright red and gold in the fall sunshine, Phoebe was still asking herself those questions. She was not asking them of anyone else, though. Since those early days in Lexington and Concord and Boston, battles had been fought all through the thirteen colonies, and people had become frightened, uncertain about who was friend and who foe. There were stories of families — children and adults alike — being hounded from their homes, injured, and even killed, by neighbours who called them enemies, sometimes in the name of the King, sometimes in the name of the rebellious Continental Congress. In this year, 1777, there was fierce fighting in lower New York Province and on the western side of Vermont's own Green Mountains, at Hubbardton and Bennington. No battles had yet been fought on the eastern side of the mountains — Orland Village was still peaceful. All the same, the war had invaded the lives of the settlers there, as everywhere in America.

Only a few months earlier, Vermont had declared itself an independent republic, but, all the same, people in this new republic were as divided in their feelings about the war as were people everywhere. Neighbours, friends, families here, too, had turned against one another, although a few, like Josiah Robinson, believed too strongly in peace to take either side. Village life had changed. Families no longer gathered for house- or barn-raisings. Gone now was the easy way in which Master Jonas Marsh, the Orland Village blacksmith, would have forged a pair of door hinges for Master Philip Grantham, the miller, and be willing to wait for his pay until the grain was ready for grinding. Gone was the way Mistress Mary Converse had offered her bread starter when Mistress Deborah Williams had let hers run out. Never quite sure which side of the rebellion a family inclined to — unless the men had gone off to fight on one side or the other — people feared to be too friendly. Up and down the rutted path through the village, doors were shut against known British sympathizers. Only Polly Grantham remained friendly towards the Robinsons.

Phoebe knew that some of the Orland Village men had formed a Committee of Public Safety — as in other villages sympathetic to the rebellion — to ensure loyalty to the rebel cause. They called themselves Patriots. Those, like Gideon, who stayed with the King called themselves Loyalists, though the Patriots called them Tories, an old British word for supporters of the king. As for those who wanted nothing to do with the war — the Patriots figured they were Tories, too.

On the village green there was a great oak tree — a tree too splendid to be felled, the villagers had decided when they had first cut through the forest to make their settlement. This, the Committee of Public Safety labelled their "Liberty Tree." Every village and town in the thirteen rebellious colonies had a liberty tree, where zealous Patriots read proclamations, gave speeches, and hanged effigies of the Loyalist leaders.

The Robinsons were anxious, but until that fall there had been no violence in Orland Village. Elsewhere suspected Tories had been robbed, imprisoned, or turned from their homes to make their way, if they could, through the deep wilderness to find refuge in British strongholds. Some, it was said, to take ship to Halifax, in Nova Scotia, the fourteenth American colony, where the rebellion had not taken hold, or to head up the river to Canada, where the conquered French took no part in the revolution. Some people had been "tarred and feathered" — stripped naked, covered with hot pine pitch, and rolled in chicken feathers until their skin peeled, then carried out of town clinging to fence rails. News of these horrors had been reaching the village with every traveller coming up the river or over the mountains.

Then, very early one clear, cold October morning not long after the first light snowfall, when the sun had only just risen over the flaming red of the maple trees, the quiet of the village was shattered by sounds of shouting. Jed and Noah rushed outside to see what had happened. Phoebe was right behind them, intent on getting them back into the house to finish their breakfast, but when she heard what was happening she was so shocked she forgot about the boys.

"We don't need the likes of traitors like you in our God-fearing village!" It was Elihu Pickens, the head of the Committee of Public Safety. He was pulling Deborah Williams through her front doorway. Phoebe caught sight of Asa Johnson behind her, and there were others barely discernible in the dim house — other members of the committee, she knew. The Williams's hound, Scout, crouched by the door, growling. People farther down the road were clutching shawls, thrusting arms into coats, shoving hats onto their heads as they hurried to the scene. Phoebe caught sight of Polly Grantham being pulled along by her mother. She could see how frightened the girl was.

John Williams, his wife, Deborah, and their five children, lived across the road from the blacksmith shop, only three houses away from the Robinsons. Now the Williams's cart, the ox harnessed to the front, was pulled up to the door. Moses Litchfield and Hiram Jesse were shoving the four small Williams children, wide-eyed with bewilderment, into the cart. With one hand Deborah clung to her door jamb. She held her baby tightly in her other arm. Her usually neatly pinned brown hair hung loose around her face and her clothes were in disarray. It was clear she had been dressing when the men had forced their way into her house.

"No!" she cried. "You can't set me out of my own house. Where will we go? We'll starve!"

"Starve if you must," jeered Elihu Pickens, "that ain't no never mind of ourn. We been generous. We let you have a sack of beans, a sack of flour, and a cooking pot. We gived you yer bible and yer fancy clock you set such store by, and blankets and such so's you won't up and freeze. What's more, we gived you yer marriage lines so's you can be legal up there with them monseers in Canaday or in Novy Scotey or wherever you fetches up."

With these words Pickens pried her hand from the door jamb and shoved her towards the cart. Deborah Williams was small, she had no chance of winning a battle of strength against a big, burly man like Elihu Pickens. She climbed, almost fell, into the cart.

"Aw, she don't need that fancy clock." Moses Litchfield grabbed the tall case clock from little Margaret Williams, who was trying desperately to get her arms around it. She burst into tears and started to climb down from the cart to take it back. Litchfield gave her a shove.

"Easy there." Jonas Marsh, the blacksmith, spoke up from across the road. "Whatever they've a-done, Mose Litchfield, you got no call for to hurt them little ones. You got no right to steal their clock, neither."

"You a Tory-lover, Jonas Marsh?" Litchfield spat in Marsh's direction. "You a-wantin' to keep yer friends company?"

There was an indignant murmur from the crowd. Hiram Jesse gave the ox a slap on the rump that started it moving. The cart wheels creaked. Deborah Williams, clutching her baby to her breast, sat stony-faced at the front of the cart. Her jaw was rigid, her eyes looked straight ahead. The terrified children behind her clung to each other soundlessly. The hound, with one final growl, jumped up into the cart beside the children.

Anne and Aunt Rachael had come up behind Phoebe. Anne turned a white face to her. "It's because John Williams is said to be off fighting for the King, isn't it?" she whispered. When Phoebe did not respond at once, Anne grabbed her by the shoulder. "It is, isn't it? Isn't it?"

"Yes. Yes, I expect so." Phoebe shivered.

Deborah's husband, John, had disappeared a few months earlier, and a lot of people believed that he had gone to join a Loyalist regiment or was spying for the British. It did not matter that Deborah told her neighbours he had had word that his mother back in Massachusetts was very ill and he had packed his necessaries and gone off at once.

"But Phoebe, only last month Elihu Pickens ——"

"Hush!" Before Anne could say anything more, Phoebe slipped her hand over her cousin's mouth. With her other hand she dragged her frantically up the road and into their house. Aunt Rachael was right behind. Jed and Noah, for once, had nothing to say. They followed their mother into the house without a sound. Aunt Rachael closed the door firmly behind her. Anne turned on Phoebe.

"Don't you dare put your hand over my mouth," she cried. "If I want to speak out, I will speak out. You're a little coward, Phoebe Olcott. Well, I am not. I am not afraid and, what's more, I'd like to upset that Elihu Pickens — and Moses Litchfield and Hiram Jesse, too. Stealing Deborah Williams's clock! That was her mama's clock. And what of all her other things and her house and…and…nobody in this whole village doing a thing to stop them!" Anne's face was as red as autumn sumac. "Oh, them and their Committee of Public Safety! I know what bug got up Elihu Pickens's nose and, if I want to shout that he was trying to court Deborah Williams whilst her husband was away, I will!"

"Anne" — Aunt Rachael's tone did not allow for argument — "Phoebe is right. This is no time to be shouting words like that out where people can hear you. She's thinking about Gideon, and so should you be. Remember where your brother is. No one knows for certain where John Williams is. The poor man might be with his mother, or he might be drowned in the river. Or he might be off serving in Pennsylvania with George Washington himself. But everyone knows where Gideon is. He made no secret of where he was going. It's not safe for people in our perilous position to rile men like Elihu Pickens."

"But they wouldn't..." Anne's voice quavered.

"They well might." Her mother sighed. "And there is not a living, breathing soul in this village who could or would stop them. We saw what happened to Deborah Williams and her children. No one is safe. If Jonas Marsh were not the only blacksmith in the village, who knows what might have happened to him merely for speaking out like a decent human being. Come, children, we must eat breakfast." Aunt Rachael took the silent boys by their hands and walked purposefully into the keeping-room, heading towards the kitchen. The orange cat meowed loudly at Phoebe, then followed Aunt Rachael and the boys.

"I hate this war," cried Anne. She flung herself

into the hard ladder-back chair that stood in the hallway. "When men like Elihu Pickens get to turn everything upside down. Nothing is any good now. The boys have all gone off like beef-wits to fight in their sacred war. Even stupid Gershom Lake has gone." She burst into tears, wiped them away angrily with her fists, sniffed, and fled up the stairs to her bedroom, for once not thinking about what effect she might have on anyone else.

Phoebe hugged herself against the fear. "What will Deborah Williams do out in the cold, frosty nights with all those children? It *can't* be right," she whispered.

That afternoon Phoebe did what she had not done for months. She packed herself a bit of bread and meat and went to spend a few hours alone in her old home. The day had gotten warmer and there was little wind. The whole trip down the hill along Trout Brook, across the meadow to where Gideon's canoe was pulled up in the reeds by the river edge, and across the dark water, took scarcely an hour. She stood outside her own cabin door for a minute or two, think-ing about her father, the pain of missing him turning her suddenly dizzy. He had been such a dreamer to think he could make a good soldier, a man whose mind was always lost in his books.

She pushed open the door. And froze. In the dimness of the room, she saw a man standing at the single table, his back to her. At the sound of the opening door, he spun around. He had a knife gripped in his hand.

"Gideon!" Phoebe sagged against the door jamb.

"Shut the door," he whispered. "For God's sake, shut the door."

"Gideon?" Phoebe moved into the room. She shoved the door closed behind her, staring, stunned, at him. Her heart was pounding violently. She couldn't think.

He stuck the knife into the sheath at his waist, then took a step towards her. "I didn't mean to frighten you, Mouse." His voice was still a hoarse whisper. "But, if I were to be found here like this, I'd be done for."

"But Gideon, what...?"

"Don't ask me anything, Phoebe. Oh, but it is good to see you!" In two steps he had reached her, lifted her off her feet, and squeezed her until she cried out.

"Oh, Phoebe." He set her back on the floor. "I have missed you all so much. You must tell me all the news. How is Mother? Father? Anne? the little ones? And Polly, what of Polly Grantham? Phoebe, is she...has...is she courting another?" He asked this last so softly Phoebe had to strain to hear him.

"No. Polly turned away Seth Andrews. She keeps to herself. She's afraid now because everyone in the village is so against the Loyalists. Seth has gone off to fight with the rebels. So have Gershom Lake and Ephraim Lewis and the Thatchers — the father and all the sons but Jake. He's gone with the British. There aren't any young men left at home. We girls have to tend to the livestock now, and the farming as well as the housework."

"Oh, Phoebe," Gideon groaned. "I so long to see her — or even get word to her. I know I oughtn't. I know but… " Gideon began to pace around the room.

Phoebe said nothing. She was still in a state of shock at finding him there. And it was so soon after the terrible thing that had happened to Deborah Williams and her children. What was he doing here? He was so distraught. And so changed. He had grown taller, thinner. Thinner, she supposed, was what happened even in the British army, which, by all reports, was better off than the half-starved American army. But it was more than that. Gideon's face, which had always shown on it every thought in his head, was tight and closed. And there was something else. She realized, suddenly, that Gideon was not dressed as a soldier. He had on a woodsman's fringed deerskin leggings and shirt, and there were moccasins on his feet. Only his hair, braided and tied back in its neat queue, suggested the soldier.

"Gideon," she asked timidly, "are you not in the army?"

"Yes, yes, of course, I am." He stopped his pacing to stand before her. "But, Phoebe, it is not at all what I thought." There was a bitter note in his voice. "The British don't think much of their loyal Americans. We're all rude backwoodsmen to them, a pack of know-nothings. I don't believe the King over in London cares as much as a flyspeck about any of us. If I had known... " He fell silent.

"But why are you dressed like a woodsman?"

"God in Heaven, Phoebe, it'd be my death to go skulking through the woods in uniform."

All at once Phoebe was aware of how cold and dark the room was. She didn't understand what Gideon meant, not really, but she knew one thing. "You must leave, Gideon. You must not stay here," she entreated. "We all know what happens to soldiers found out of uniform by their enemies. Gideon, they are hanged!" She shivered. "Why have you come here? You cannot know how bad things are now for Tories." She told him about Deborah Williams. "And no one dared lift a hand to help her. Everyone is frightened of Elihu Pickens and his committee. Go away, Gideon! Go away!"

"I know." Gideon sighed. He started up his pacing again. "I did not know about the Williamses, but I know how it is for us Loyalists almost everywhere in Vermont and New Hampshire. I guess I should be glad I didn't ask Polly to marry me. No one will bother her. And you are all safe because of your father. Oh that this war would end!" His voice broke. He came back abruptly to stand before Phoebe. "Will you do something for me?" He took her hand.

Phoebe was filled with sudden alarm. She knew Gideon was going to ask for something she was not going to want to do, and she was just as sure she was going to do it. Her shoulders slumped.

"I want you to take a letter to Polly Grantham."

Phoebe didn't answer at once. She had a terrible feeling that what Gideon wanted was dangerous — that it could bring him nothing but harm.

"Phoebe, will you take the letter?"

She still said nothing.

"Will you?"

"If I take the letter, will you go away? Don't come near Orland Village. Don't try to see Polly. I'll take the letter and you'll go from here." She knew there was pleading in her voice when she so wanted firmness, but she couldn't help it.

"Yes. Yes, I will." Gideon turned at once to Phoebe's father's desk in the corner by the window. There he rummaged in its cubby-holes until he found a sheet of paper and a bit of a lead pencil.

It was late afternoon by this time. Day was fading fast. What little light there was was filtered through the months of dust and dirt collected on the glass of the single window. Gideon wasn't much more than a dark shadow hunched over the desk. The dark figure, the sense of fear and sadness around him, reminded Phoebe of a picture in one of her father's books of Thomas More writing his last words in the tower of London before his head was to come off. Phoebe shuddered. "Gideon, do not write the letter." She started towards him, but he turned then and pressed the folded paper into her hand.

"If you will take this to Polly, Mouse, I will be in your debt for ever."

Phoebe did not have the heart to say she would not. She could do nothing else for him and he wanted so badly to reach Polly.

"Mind" — he fixed her with a fierce look — "you are not to let on, not to anyone but Polly, that you have seen me. Not anyone. Not even my mother. Remember what I say. It'll mean my death if these rebels find me. So I'm for the woods again, dear little Mouse — and thank you," he added softly.

Phoebe was so frightened by the thought of what might happen to him that she couldn't say anything. She threw her arms around him and kissed him. Then, with the note to Polly Grantham gripped in her hand, she left him.

All the way home, until it was way too dark, she was tempted to read what Gideon had written. She couldn't bring herself to pry into his thoughts and feelings — she loved him too much for that. But had he, as she so feared, asked Polly to meet him somewhere? Would he risk that?

It was fully dark by the time she reached Orland Village. There was no one around, no one to see her creep silently up to the Granthams' house at the top of the hill by the brook, no one to see her edge her way towards the woodpile, where, by good fortune, Polly was getting logs for the fire; no one to see the quick, furtive exchange of words or paper, no one to see her slip along the road to the Robinsons' house.

When Anne asked her crossly where she had been all afternoon, Phoebe said truthfully that she had gone "over home" but told her no more.

"You left Jed and Noah with no one but me to look out for them. What kept you until past supper time?" Anne demanded. Phoebe mumbled something about having to make sure the hearth fire was doused. She could not tell Anne about Gideon because she had promised. She was heartsick to have to keep her knowledge from Aunt Rachael and Uncle Josiah, knowing that for them to even hear he was alive would light up their faces with happiness.

All evening she tried to concentrate on Uncle Josiah's Bible reading, but she could think only of Gideon. How she wished she had read what he'd written in his letter! Did he mean to try to see Polly? He had said he would leave, but, she remembered, he had not looked her in the eye. Now she was sure it was what he had meant to do.

The lump of fear in her throat grew until she could barely swallow. She needed all her willpower to keep from jumping up and crying out for someone to stop Gideon from coming to the village to see Polly. But she didn't do that. She sat still in her straight ladder-back chair, her hands busy with her knitting, with George, the orange cat, asleep by her feet. She appeared, she hoped, to have no thoughts in her head but those arising from her uncle's reading.

Later she lay stiff and wakeful in the big spool bed beside a sleeping Anne. Gideon's words, "It'll mean my death if I am found," echoing over and over in her head in a macabre chant.

It wasn't much past dawn when the knock came on the door. Aunt Rachael went to open it. It was Billy Wilder. His high, thin wail pierced the silence of the house. "Oh...oh... oh...m-m-m-mistress," he cried, "th-th-they strung him up, oh...oh...oh...ohh!"

Aunt Rachael pulled him into the house and

tried to get him to sit down, but he only tugged at her hand and she could get no sense from him. In the end, she pried her hand loose and left him with Uncle Josiah while she dressed hastily. In a very few moments the whole family — Aunt Rachael, Uncle Josiah, Anne, her shawl trailing after her, and the little boys, still half asleep — were hurrying after the howling figure running down the road towards the village green.

Only Phoebe stayed behind. She knew. The moment she heard the sound of Billy's voice, she knew. Standing at the top of the stairs, looking down at him, she turned cold, then dizzy. Then a kind of calm settled over her. Methodically, almost ceremonially, she put on her shift, her petticoat, her skirt, her blouse, and her warm waistcoat. She pulled on her stockings and put her feet into her shoes. Then she brushed and braided her hair. She wrapped her shawl around her shoulders and walked slowly and steadily towards the village green.

Under the great oak tree in the centre of The Green, with its crude "Liberty Tree" label, she could see a dark mass of people in the early light. The Robinson family was huddled together at its edge. A stout rope had been slung over a branch about eight feet from the ground. Gideon's lifeless body was hanging from the rope. On his shirt a note was pinned. It read: "Death to all Traitors and Spies."

CHAPTER 3

The Message

The note on Gideon's shirt fluttered in the morning breeze. Someone behind Phoebe screamed. Fists pounded on her back. The screaming was in her ears, words she didn't understand. She made herself turn around. Anne's face was red and twisted, her eyes wide, her mouth wider, and her voice one high shriek. Anne's fists came at her face.

"You did this. You and your father and his rebel friends! You did this. You miserable traitor. It's all your fault!" Her screams rose higher and higher. Her fists pounded and pounded on Phoebe's face, her chest, her arms. Phoebe was so stunned she could not even think to put her hands up to protect herself. The shrill, almost inhuman sound went on and on. "You did it! You did it! Go away from here and never come back! Go! Go! Go!"

Someone pulled Anne away from her. Phoebe raised her head. She looked around her at her cousin, at all the other people, with a feeling of such distance it was as though she had never seen any of them before, the tall woman standing so stiff and still, her face as grey as wood ash; the thin, trembling man, clinging to her sleeve, the little boys, their faces, so white, lifted to the lifeless body on the tree, the thrashing, screaming girl, her arms held behind her by someone's strong hands; the silent crowd behind them. A shattering sob began somewhere inside Phoebe. She spun around, then ran as though the vengeance of God were chasing her along the road and down the hill. She stopped when suddenly she found the river at her feet. She threw herself down at the foot of the big willow tree. Great wracking sobs shook her until she had not the strength for any more. Then she crawled to the edge of the river. She splashed her face over and over again and then drank the clear, cold water. She drew a deep, shuddering breath. She sat by the water, trying to take in all that had happened, but all she could think of, all she could see, was Gideon's body hanging from the Liberty Tree.

"If only I had said I wouldn't take the letter to Polly Grantham," she moaned over and over, rocking back and forth in an agony of grief and guilt. "I knew it wasn't safe. He said that himself,

'It'll be my death if I am found.' Oh, Gideon!"
She put her head down on her knees and wept
again.

Much later, and only gradually, she began to
hear the sounds of the world around her: the
soft chirping of finches and chickadees, the gentle washing of the river against the shore, the
insistent chattering of a squirrel, the cawing of
crows. She lifted her head and saw that the sun
was well up in the sky. There was a stiff breeze,
making the tender, supple willow branches sway
and wafting the odour of fish from the river.
Phoebe realized that she was cold. She tucked
her feet under her and wiped the tears on her
face with her sleeve. She looked up at the big red
squirrel sitting on a low branch of the tree. His
tail was twitching and he was scolding angrily.

"Hello, Constant." Phoebe sighed. "Why
are you scolding me? There's naught in your
house to fret about — not anymore. Look, I'll
show you." She thrust her hand into the hollow.
Her fingers touched something that was not
Constant's stash of nuts. Surprised, she pulled it
out. It was a tiny silk packet — small enough to
fit into a walnut shell, she thought. She reached
her hand into the hollow again and felt around.
There was another scrap of paper. On it was a
note written in lead pencil. "If I am discovered,
get this message to the Mohawk Elias Brant, in
Hanover." It was signed with the letter G.

Phoebe turned the packet over and over in her hands. "Small enough to fit inside a walnut shell," she said aloud — or, the thought came swiftly and unbidden, inside the queue of a man's hair. And there was the memory of Gideon the day he had marched proudly off to join a Loyalist regiment. The sun had been as bright as this day's sun, shining on his brown hair, braided and tied with a plain black ribbon. Yesterday she had paid no heed to his hair, but that queue was clear in her mind now, and how the tell-tale packet she held in her suddenly sweaty hand could have fitted into it.

She realized then what she should have realized the day before (only the day before?). Gideon had been dressed in deerskin leggings and shirt, and not in uniform. "He was a spy," she whispered. "He was. Oh, Gideon, why did you have to come here?" But she knew the answer to that, too. Whatever his errand may have been, wherever he'd been going, he hadn't been able to keep himself from slipping through the woods to see Polly Grantham.

Phoebe looked down at the packet through the tears that would start up again. Almost without thinking, she pulled at the thread that held it together until it came loose. With trembling fingers she opened it. There were two sheets of onion-skin paper. On the top one was a message. It was addressed to Brigadier-General

43

Watson Powell at Fort Ticonderoga, in New York. Phoebe could not understand another word. She looked at it blankly. Then she looked at the second sheet of paper. There were perfectly plain English words on it: "Please offer protection to the three New York families living south of Skenesborough, near Wood Creek, the families of Loyalist soldiers Jethro Colliver, Septimus Anderson, and Charles Morrissay." It was signed with an initial Phoebe couldn't decipher. She stared at first the one page, then the other, in a kind of trance. She read the second page again. She studied the first page. Then it came to her.

"It's in code," she said. She looked around her furtively, fearing she might have been overheard. Quickly she refolded the papers into the tiny square they had been in and squeezed them into their bag.

What am I to do with this, she asked herself. First she thought she would tear it into bits and throw it into the river, because she didn't want anything to do with this message that had been to blame for Gideon's death, but the words "protection for the families" leapt into her mind. She thought of Deborah Williams and her children.

I cannot leave those other families to that fate. I cannot. I must take this to Elias Brant, she thought. But then she remembered that Elias was no longer in Hanover. All the Mohawk students had gone to fight with the British. She had heard Gershom Lake and John Barber talking about them in front of the blacksmith shop one evening when she and Anne had been walking home from a day's quilting at Mistress Shipley's. "Wal, you can't expect loyalty from no Indian," Gershom was saying. He had sneered at them as they walked past. "Never mind them savages." He'd looked sideways at Anne. "It's them others. Anyone with kin fighting for those damned redcoats had better have good friends on the right side of this war." Anne had tossed her head and sniffed, and the girls had walked on. Phoebe had thought about her father's Mohawk student Peter Sauk, who called her Little Bird and had brought her moccasins his mother had made. She wondered if he might be fighting somewhere with Gideon. He would be a good friend to Gideon.

But, like Peter Sauk, Elias Brant had gone off to fight — he was not in Hanover to take Gideon's message.

What was she to do? Take it to Aunt Rachael? What could Aunt Rachael do? But the only answer she got was the sound of Constant, the squirrel, nibbling intently on a beechnut she held tightly in her paws. "And it *is* my fault. I should never have taken the letter to Polly. Never. I knew, I just knew, he meant to see her."

She put her head down on her knees again, her heart in turmoil.

At last she grew quiet. "Well" — she sniffed — "I'll just have to take it to Fort Ticonderoga myself." She sat up straight. "But Fort Ticonderoga is on the other side of the mountains. It's on the other side of Lake Champlain. In New York. I can't go there."

From somewhere inside her the words came: "Yes, you can. You can do it for Gideon. You can show Anne you're not a traitor."

"I'm not a traitor! I know I'm not a traitor," Phoebe cried, answering that voice. "I'm not a rebel and I'm not a Tory. I don't know what I am. Just because Papa was for the revolution, do I have to be? Oh, Papa, why did you have to go off like that, and now Gideon." She broke down again, the tears streaming down her cheeks into the collar of her dress.

"I don't know what I am and I can't go over the mountains all by myself."

"Then who will do it?" asked that voice. "I don't know," she answered. Back and forth, back and forth went the argument in her mind until she put her tired head down on her knees once more and fell asleep.

The sun was setting when she woke. She remembered everything. She shivered from the cold and from the bleakness, but she felt more peaceful. Somehow, while she slept, a decision had been made. She knew what she had to do. Stiffly she stood up. She kilted up her skirt and put the message in her pocket. She smoothed her clothes with her hands, then undid her braid and did it up again. She washed her face and drank again from the river. Then, with new purpose in her every move, she went to Gideon's canoe, still pulled up on shore where she had left it the night before, shoved it into the water, and set out across the river.

Back in her own home, she searched for the rough map one of her father's students had once drawn for her of New Hampshire and Vermont. He had wanted to show her his home on the Onion River, near Lake Champlain, and the way he had travelled to Hanover along the military road leading from the lake over the mountains to the Connecticut River. She had stored it in one of the desk's cubby-holes. The map was not where she had always kept it. The only thing in the drawer was the tinder-box her father had forgotten to take with him. She picked it up. Then she realized that the map must have been the paper on which Gideon had written his letter. She took from her pocket the scrap with the hastily scribbled note he had left in the hollow tree. Sure enough, on the back of it were the lines showing the Connecticut River, where the White River emptied into it, and the easternmost part of the military road. She stared at it, heartsick.

She searched frantically through the desk, under it, around the room, but the other half of the map was nowhere to be found. "Now what will I do?" she asked aloud, as though she hoped someone would appear by a miracle to answer. The miracle occurred. Gideon's voice came into her head as clear and sure as it had been that day in the woods so long ago, when she'd asked him where Trout Brook began.

"All you have to do to get across the mountains, Phoebe," he said, "is follow our brook west, because that's where it comes from. I mean to follow it one day, all the way to Lake Champlain." Then he had laughed.

"And now it is I who will go to Lake Champlain." Phoebe spoke the words softly, like a promise to the memory of Gideon still so alive in this room where he had paced and paced only a day ago.

She did not weep as she thought this. There did not seem to be any tears left. A calm had settled over her — not the cold calm she had felt when the certainty of Gideon's death had come to her, but the calm that came of absolute determination. She knew what she was going to do and how she was going to do it. She wished she could leave without going back to the Robinsons' house. She did not want to lie to Aunt Rachael, and she could not tell her what she meant to do, because Aunt Rachael would certainly stop her from going. And she could not bear to face Anne, but she needed her mother's warm cloak and something to eat. Taking one last look around the room, Phoebe went outside and latched the door carefully after her.

CHAPTER 4

I Will Need to be
Very Brave

Dusk was deepening by the moment. The last of the rosy sunset hung over the deep green hills across the river, and the moon was not yet up, when Phoebe started down the Hanover hill. It had snowed a little, and a wind was coming up. Holding her shawl tightly around her, she hurried to keep warm and to keep from hearing the scuffling of wild animals in the wet leaves. She didn't mind the pigeons cooing in the branches overhead or the plaintive sound of a late whip-poor-will somewhere in the trees, but the thought of wolves and wild cats made her shudder. Then, halfway down the hill, she heard a twig snap behind her. Someone was following her. She raced the rest of the way down the hill, jumped into the canoe, and pushed off from shore.

Out on the river, well away from shore, she stopped paddling and forced herself to look back. There was no sign of anyone. There were only the branches of the alders and willows swaying silently in the wind. She rested back on her heels in the canoe and let the current carry her for a moment until she realized that she could soon be a mile down river unless she started to paddle. She looked into the deep, black water. She jumped and almost lost her paddle when she heard a beaver slap its tail somewhere along the river bank. How was she ever going to face the unknown wilderness for days and days — and nights — when she was this frightened of the part of it she knew so well?

"I will need to be brave," she whispered to the night. "I will need to be very brave." But Phoebe had never felt brave, and she had never ventured beyond her own home, other than along the route between Hanover and Orland Village, and a small distance into the woods with Gideon on his plant quests.

She dipped her paddle resolutely into the water. When she reached the shore, she pulled the canoe up by the willow trees and tried not to think about how long it might be before she did that again. She made her way silently along the brook up the hill and the several hundred yards along the road to the village green. There she stopped. And fell silent. She could not make herself walk past the tree where Gideon's body had hung.

Gideon's body. She had not been thinking about Gideon's body. It would be laid out in the Robinsons' parlour. The family would be there, watching over it. She swallowed back hot tears. She stood at the edge of The Green, irresolute. She wanted to be there with them, keeping vigil. Even more, she wanted to run away and never return to this place of grief and misery. She felt that she could do neither. She could not tell Aunt Rachael what she meant to do, but realized now that she could not leave without some kind of goodbye. And she knew she had to get something to eat and her warm cloak. When she thought about food, she realized that she had had none since supper the night before and that then she had eaten almost nothing because she had been so upset about Gideon's letter to Polly.

Suddenly the hair rose on the back of her neck. A dark shape moved in the shadows of the trees at the edge of The Green. There was someone there. She knew there was. She froze. It was now so dark she could barely distinguish one tree from another, but she could see eyes, and the only sound she heard was Trout Brook in the distance, burbling over the stones on its way down the hill.

"Is someone there?" whispered Phoebe. There was no reply. She shivered, looked around again, and pulled her shawl so tightly around her shoulders she felt it strain. She edged around the village green, turning only once to peer over her shoulder, and went along the road to Mistress Shipley's cabin. There she slipped behind the cabins to the Robinsons' back door. Only Quincy, Moses Litchfield's old dog, noticed her passing. He growled once, but settled back at the sound of her familiar voice.

Gratefully she sank down onto the stone step, not bothering to brush the thin layer of snow from it. Within seconds, she felt an impatient nudging at her hip. She looked down. It was the cat. George was bad-tempered and demanding, and seemed to care for no one, except that he had let Phoebe — and only Phoebe — feed him. He had never before sat down beside her. She reached over to stroke him. He hissed, but he did not get up. A moment later Phoebe did. Her head ached from fatigue, from weeping, from making and unmaking decisions, and from hunger. She lifted the latch on the back door very quietly and let herself into the house.

There was no one in the kitchen, and the only light came from the low-burning wood fire on the grate in the big fireplace. Its homey, acrid odour welcomed her. The remains of the evening meal had been laid by on the dresser. Phoebe cut herself a bit of ham with the paring knife that lay beside the plate, and a square of johnnycake, but, after two bites, she put it down.

She took off her shoes and went on tiptoe to the front hall. She started up the stairs. She did not want to go into the parlour. She did not want to look into that room. But George gave her away. He had followed her so closely that she stepped on his foot. He let out a squawk.

"Is that you, Phoebe?" Aunt Rachael came to the doorway. For a moment they stood there without moving, Phoebe with one foot poised to start up the stairs, Aunt Rachael, tall and still, her face ghostly grey behind the flickering light of her candle.

"Where were — " she began.

"I was — " Phoebe started to say.

They both stopped.

"It doesn't matter," said Aunt Rachael. "You are here now. Come." She took Phoebe by the hand, and Phoebe had no choice but to follow her into the parlour.

There, under the front window, was the pine box resting on a pair of saw-horses, the scent of the fresh wood still strong. Phoebe couldn't help but wonder who in the village had been bold enough to make a coffin for a Loyalist soldier. At either end of it a candle burned brightly in Aunt Rachael's best pewter candlesticks. Wrapped in a shroud, Gideon's body lay resting in the coffin. For just one instant Phoebe wanted to rip the shroud away, to look at Gideon's face once more. Then she remembered, with terrible clarity, what his face had looked like early that morning. She gripped Aunt Rachael's hand so hard that Aunt Rachael pulled it away. She put her arm around Phoebe.

Uncle Josiah stood at the far end of the coffin. His head was bowed and he was reading from the Bible in a low, steady voice. Phoebe knelt with her aunt and prayed. She tried to listen to the words Uncle Josiah was reading, but, even more, she wanted to plead with God to be kind to this boy who had loved God's world so much. It was all she could think, all she could pray about. How Gideon had treasured the plants and animals in the woods! How he wanted to know about them, to understand them! With Aunt Rachael she said the prayer for the repose of Gideon's soul. Silently, she promised him again that she would finish his work, she would take his message over the mountains to the fort.

As she stood up, she became aware that there was someone else in the room. At first she thought it was Anne and she steeled herself to face her. Then the girl moved into the light of the candle and she saw that it was Polly Grantham. Phoebe went to stand by her. They looked at each other; neither spoke, but Phoebe was sure that Polly felt, too, that they shared a terrible secret. She forced her eyes from Polly's pain-filled ones. She took her hand in a tight, quick grasp, then turned and fled the room.

Blindly she climbed the stairs to the bedroom she shared with Anne. The fire had died in the hearth and there was only the glow from the embers to see by. Carefully, she tiptoed across the room to the built-in cupboard beside the fireplace. From her corner of it, she took her moccasins and her mother's tartan wool cloak. The red glow caught the silver clasp in its light, and Phoebe had a fleeting memory of herself, very small, playing with that clasp. She closed her eyes against the pang of longing that the memory brought. Resolutely, she eased the cupboard door closed. One of the hinges squeaked and Anne woke up.

"Who's there?" Her voice was thick with sleep. She sat up. Phoebe froze. She said nothing. She waited. After a moment or two Anne lay back down, turned over, and went back to sleep. Phoebe tiptoed out of the room. In the next room one of the boys cried out. When there was no other sound, Phoebe went downstairs to the kitchen. She picked up the paring knife to cut a bit of ham, then looked at the bit she had cut earlier and forgotten. She turned away; the sight and the smell of the food had taken all her appetite from her. She stuffed her feet into her moccasins, put her mother's warm cloak around her over her shawl, squatted down to say good-bye to George, looked around her once more, and slid out the door.

As silently as she had come, she skirted the village street, past the backs of the houses, through barnyards to the brook, bubbling and splashing over the stones, glistening under the stars and a crescent moon. How she longed to follow it down the hill to the river, to go home to Hanover to her own house, to shut the door and never come out. But she had made her mind up. She had made a promise to Gideon. She looked down at the brook.

"This is the way Gideon said to go," she whispered, "he said to follow the brook west, so that is what I will have to do."

She turned her steps to the west, up the hill, against the down-rush of the brook, and started forth.

CHAPTER 5

Alone

It was a little over fifty miles through the dense wilderness and over high mountains from the Connecticut River to Lake Champlain, where Fort Ticonderoga lies. For a strong, full-grown man, wise in the ways of the woods, it was at least a week's journey. Phoebe was strong, but she was not quite fifteen, not very tall, and a little plump. What's more, she had not travelled any farther than Orland Village from Hanover since she'd gone there to live at the age of nine. She had listened, though, because she loved him, to Gideon's long-winded lectures on woodland life and to her father's Mohawk students when they talked of home in the Mohawk River valley, in New York, because they spoke of it so glowingly.

But now, faced with a journey she had come to see might take weeks through dark, wild land full of dangerous animals, she wished desperately that she was an experienced hunter and that she had paid strict attention to Gideon's every word about forest plants. And winter was not far off.

She tripped over the protruding root of a big tree that grew beside a pool glinting in the moonlight, in a depression halfway up a steep hill. To her dismay, she realized Trout Brook went no farther. She had barely begun her journey and she had reached the end of the brook. She heard again in her tired mind Gideon's voice. "I mean to follow it one day all the way to Lake Champlain." And then he had laughed. She hadn't paid attention to that laugh. Gideon had known Trout Brook would never lead all the way over the high mountains to Lake Champlain — of course, he had. How stupid she felt! Her feet were wet, and she was shivering inside her cloak, despite its warm fur lining. She felt as though she had been running, crawling, stumbling along and into Trout Brook for ever. Once or twice she had lost it because the little light the crescent moon shed did not reach far into the deep woods. Then her ear would pick up the bubbling sound of it as it tumbled over rocks or her foot would slip into it. And now she had come to the end of it.

She dropped beside the pool. "Oh, Father in heaven," she moaned, "I will surely perish out here in the wild, of cold or hunger or because a wolf or a catamount will take me."

There was a sudden rustling in the leaves under a tall bush about a foot from her. She sat up. The hair stood up on the back of her neck. The rustling grew louder. The head of a large house cat emerged from the bush. Phoebe stared at it, weak with relief.

"George?"

His eyes were two glowing coals in the dark. He did not move, but Phoebe knew by the way he thrust his head forward so belligerently that it was George.

"What are you doing here, George?" She reached for him. He darted up a tree, perched himself on a branch just out of reach, and turned his back to her.

"Stay there, then. I am much too tired to even try to fetch you down." She lay down, rolled her shawl up and put it under her head, pulled her cloak over her, and fell asleep with the soft gurgling sound of the brook in her ear.

She woke, hours later, to see an arrow of sunlight strike a patch of leaves on the ground in front of her. On that bright patch a chipmunk stood on its hind legs, rigid with fear. George crouched, inches away, ready to pounce. Phoebe shot out her hand and grabbed the chipmunk. George's tail lashed angrily. For a second he looked as though he might lunge at her. Then he stalked off. She stroked the chipmunk with her finger along its black stripe. "I think you will do nicely now," she murmured. She lifted her hand. The chipmunk scooted from her lap, leapt onto a nearby log, chittered rapidly at her, then disappeared under the log.

Phoebe got up stiffly. She found a place to pee. She washed her hands and face in the pool, then cupped her hands and drank deeply from the icy water. She shook out her cloak and shawl and put them around her, looking down rue-fully at a rent in her skirt. She sat down and took off her wet stockings and her moccasins. She was glad she had thought to exchange her shoes for the moccasins. "Better in the woods — they make you more sure-footed and make less noise," Gideon had said approvingly when Peter Sauk brought them to her in thanks for so many dinners.

Dinner. Phoebe did not want to think about dinner. She realized, as she hung her stockings over a bush to dry, that she felt brighter for her drink and her wash in the pool but that she was very hungry. How she wished she had brought with her that ham and johnnycake she had spurned in Aunt Rachael's kitchen. What was she to do? She knew she had to eat. She looked around her as though a well-stocked larder might suddenly appear among the trees and bushes.

It's hopeless, she thought. It truly is hopeless. I will have to go back.

Go back. It was, at the same time, a wonderful and a dreadful idea. Anne might already be sorry she had screamed at her and hit her. Anne's hysteria never lasted very long. And Aunt Rachael would be needing help with the boys. And, oh, the sorrow would not seem so unbearable among the others who had loved Gideon. But, if she went back, she would fail Gideon again and could never atone for having carried that accursed letter to Polly Grantham. And those families who names were on that list would lose everything. No, she could not go back.

But, I must eat, she realized all too painfully, and I must plan. She leaned against a tree while she took stock of her situation. There wasn't much to take stock of. She had no spare clothes, no provisions or cooking utensils. She had no map to help her find her direction. She had two things: in her pocket she had the tinder-box she had taken from her father's desk and, amazingly, she had left Orland Village with Aunt Rachael's paring knife gripped tightly in one hand. Through all those long hours climbing the hills beside Trout Brook she had never let go of it. It had lain beside her while she slept and was there now, on the ground where she had left it. She moved over and picked it up.

"I have a knife," she crowed. "I have a knife. With a knife I can make a hook, and with a hook, and a stick and a length of vine, I can catch fish."

The pool was like a large, deep basin, with tiny streamlets trickling into it from above and Trout Brook pouring out of it over the rocks below. And there were fish. As soon as the thought of catching them struck Phoebe, she saw the fish, then wondered how she had not really noticed them earlier. There were trout and they were moving like shadows deep among the rock caves and passages under the clear water. She thought, as she had often done before, how beautiful a trout was, red and green and silver, luminous, as she'd always imagined jewels to be. It was a shame to have to catch one. But she was very hungry, so she set to work at once to fashion the hook and then find a stick and a length of vine for a rod and line. It was not difficult, it did not take long, and she was soon settled by the pool with her fishing gear.

Within minutes her first small trout was flopping on the ground. Almost at once she had three more. Quickly she gathered a pile of twigs and leaves and, with the help of the flint and steel from her tinder-box, kindled a flame. She set the fish over the fire on a little stick frame. They smelled so good cooking that she ate them burnt on the outside, raw on the inside, spitting almost more bones than she consumed flesh, and not caring at all. She hardly tasted them, she ate so fast. But she felt better and not quite so cold. She was ready to resume her journey.

"I wish the sun were not so far away," she grumbled, "or, at least, that the trees were not so high, so that I could see where the sun is. Then, I think, I would know which way is west."

As if he were right there beside her, she heard again Gideon's voice explaining: "One has but to look for the moss when one is unsure of one's direction in the wild. You see, moss grows on the north side of a tree, away from the sun, always away from the sun. Spiders, to the contrary, prefer the dry, south side of a tree. Woodpeckers, particularly those great pileated woodpeckers, always tap the east side. They seem to enjoy the morning sun."

She had laughed at him. "There's no sun in the deep woods."

"Oh, indeed there is," he had assured her. "There are shadows in the forest and there is light. If you know which plants reach for the sun and which shy away from it, you can readily find your direction should you lose it. The forest is easy to read, Phoebe. You need only learn its language." He had made her repeat what he had told her. "Because, Mouse" — he had grinned at her — "you are sure to be lost in the woods if you ever grow bold enough to really venture into them."

Phoebe shook her head to clear it. She looked around her at the sunlight filtering through the deep-green pines, the golden tamaracks, and the bare branches of the hardwood trees. She listened for and heard the woodpeckers tapping, jays calling.

Glad the early snow hadn't lasted, she put her moccasins on, although they hadn't really dried in the cold air, and crunched through the dry leaves to walk slowly around the nearest trees. She inspected their bark carefully. Sure enough, here was a clump of moss on the dark side of an oak tree, and there another on the same side of a maple. And she saw woodpecker holes up and down the sides of some of the pines, and always on the sunny side.

"It's true, it's as Gideon said," she whispered. "Then this way is west — of course it is, it must be, it leads away from the brook."

Gingerly, she put on her wet stockings. She stored her tinder-box in her pocket along with her knife and the message for the General at Fort Ticonderoga. She called George. She poked around among the bushes. He had not appeared when she'd cooked the fish or come to eat the fish heads. She felt a little as though she had been abandoned, but decided that he must have gone home, that he would be better off there, that she was better off travelling without him.

She knelt beside the deep pool and said a

prayer for guidance, and another for Gideon's and her father's souls. "And," she said at the end, "please, God, help George find his way home."

Almost as a part of her prayer, she splashed water on her face and drank from the pool one last time. She said goodbye to the brook, turned, and headed towards the west.

At first she started at every rustle in the leaves, every flutter in the trees. She would peer nervously about her, sure that a wolf, a rattle-snake, or a bear was just at the point of crossing her path, but, as the day wore on, she became a little more confident. She could hear the squir-rels, chipmunks, weasels and rabbits, but she got used to them and they scurried away at the sound of her footsteps. The only large animal she saw all morning was a black bear, but it was a good distance away, across a stream, and so busy at a berry bush that it did not see her. All the same, she put her feet very carefully for a long time afterwards so as to make as little noise as possible.

She travelled all morning and well into the afternoon through dark evergreen forest where the ground was carpeted with needles that felt soft under her moccasins, the scent of pine and hemlock was heavy, and the wind soughed in the high branches. She walked through great groves of maples, oaks, and butternuts, where the sun shone brightly through the almost-bare branches. Here the jays and crows kept her company with their loud, cheerful cries, and here she found butternuts on the ground she could crack with a stone and so keep the worst of her hunger at bay.

She hiked up along swift-flowing streams and down into dark valleys. She trudged for hours up the side of a high hill, where the mountain ash grew thick, its low-hanging branches heavy with scarlet berries that gleamed against the deep-blue sky. For a time she followed a narrow but well-tramped path up a low hillside, but it ended by a pool below a waterfall where blueberries grew. She realized it must be a bear's trail and hastily retraced her steps. She knew that bears would be feeding on berries and nuts in the high ground this time of year, then looking for likely caves or hollows to hibernate in for the winter. She only hoped she wouldn't fall into a bear's chosen hollow. She recognized no Indian trails, saw no signs of human habitation, saw no more large animals except for a family of deer on the mountain where the mountain ash grew.

She found a huckleberry bush by a stream with a few berries on it the bears had missed. Greedily she stuffed them into her mouth. Then she sat down, took off her moccasins, and rubbed her tired feet. She leaned back against a large rock and listened to the rhythmic roar of the distant waterfall. After a few minutes she began to doze.

"No, I mustn't," she cried, and the sound of her own voice frightened her into wakefulness. She shoved her feet back into her moccasins. She searched the trees — probably for the fiftieth time that day — for moss and spiders and woodpecker drillings, then started off once more.

About an hour later, when the shadows had begun to lengthen across her path, Phoebe glimpsed a small meadow through the trees. She heard the growling and snarling of animals. She crept forward to the edge of the meadow. Over on the far side, by a small stream, she could see a pack of wolves tussling with something. Phoebe took a hasty step back. She felt a tree behind her. She grabbed a limb and swung herself up. Frantically, she reached for the next branch. She touched rough fur and let out a terrified squawk. The animal squawked, too, and scrambled farther up into the tree.

Oh, dear Father in Heaven, it's a catamount, Phoebe thought. Above her the animal moved. She began to pray. There was no more movement on the branch above her. Slowly she opened her eyes and looked up. A pair of terrified round black eyes looked back at her.

"You're a bear," gasped Phoebe. She almost let go of her branch, she was so frightened. Her thoughts raced: Wolves ate other animals all the time — they could eat people — bears didn't eat people, but they had such terrible claws. She looked up at the bear. She looked down and across the meadow. She could see, from this height, what the wolves were tussling over. It was the carcass of a large black bear. For a moment her stomach heaved. She took a deep breath and looked up again. The bear way above her in the tree looked quite small, not full grown. What's more, it still looked as frightened as she felt. I think I know who you are, she thought; that was your mama, wasn't it?

"I won't hurt you, if you don't hurt me," whispered Phoebe. She hiked up her skirt, wrapped her arms securely around the limb of the tree, and settled herself on the branch. A few branches above her, the bear stared down at her. It did not move. It did not make a sound.

"Bear," she whispered, after a few minutes, "we might be here all night, just the two of us, and those villains down there."

She had no sooner spoken when she heard a loud meow and a large orange cat sprang into her lap. She stifled a scream and clutched her tree branch frantically. George glared at her and dug his sharp claws into her knees.

"I was wrong," croaked Phoebe. "There are three of us. George, where did you come from? Where have you been all day?" She hugged him with one arm. He bit her. She slipped and grabbed George by his tail. He yowled and dug his claws in deeper. She managed to right herself, shaking with fright. She turned her head quickly to see if the wolves had heard the noise, but if they had they paid no attention.

They had finished with the carcass of the bear. One by one, they were loping off into the woods.

She waited a while after the last one had gone. Then, holding tightly to the cat, she eased herself from the branch and slid down the tree trunk. George jumped to the ground. Phoebe stood leaning against the tree with her head back, her eyes closed. Gradually, she sensed the presence of someone close by. She opened her eyes to see the bemused face of a tall, young Mohawk man not a foot from her.

CHAPTER 6

Peter Sauk

"Peter? Peter Sauk?" Phoebe stared at the young man in disbelief. "Peter, oh, Peter, praise God. I think I am lost again. For the first while, you see, it was clear enough that I had but to follow the brook, but then the brook came to an end, and it was because I was stupid about what Gideon said. I thought I was lost but I remembered what he said about the moss and the woodpeckers and I walked that way but then there were those wolves and there was the bear and George and...and..." She stared blankly at Peter, her thoughts a hopeless tangle.

Peter Sauk shook his head. "Little Bird," he said in the slow, deep voice Phoebe remembered from so many evenings back home in Hanover. "I don't believe I have ever heard you say so many words at once in all the years I have known you. Nor do any of them make sense. Come. It is late. My mother and my young sister are camped only a short distance from here. You will have to tell me these things later." He put his hand on her back and turned her in the direction the wolves had taken.

Phoebe did not hesitate. Peter Sauk was a person she trusted. Among the students who had spent their evenings with her father, he was one who had always greeted her with a smile and who, most often, had had a story or a joke for her, and it was he who had given her her moccasins. And here he was. Unbelievably, here he was. She didn't even stop to wonder why.

And there will be something to eat, she thought. A wonderful warmth spread through her as she followed Peter through the evening shadows. For once, George was right behind her. The bear had disappeared.

Peter was right. It took no more than a few minutes for them to cross the meadow, where Phoebe turned her face from the remains of the bear, and to find their way through the woods to a small birch glade by the edge of a river. There Peter's mother and sister had made camp. By the light of their fire, Phoebe saw the two women, dressed in deerskin leggings and tunics, busying themselves over an iron cooking pot suspended from a tripod of sticks. Whatever was in the pot smelled so good that Phoebe wanted nothing more than to sit right down with the pot in front of her and eat.

The women got to their feet as she approached. "My mother, Shakoti'nisténha." Peter bowed towards the older of the two. "My sister, Katsi'tsiénhawe." He turned to the younger, and Phoebe saw that she was a girl about her own age.

"Greetings," said Shakoti'nisténha. Katsi-'tsiénhawe stood back. She lowered her head in acknowledgement but said nothing. Peter said a few words to them in Mohawk. His mother smiled. His sister nodded shyly.

"I have told them that you are the daughter of my teacher at Dr. Wheelock's school in Hanover, the girl for whom we have been searching, also that you speak only English. Unfortunately, my sister, Katsi'tsiénhawe, speaks only Mohawk. My mother speaks only a little English. But" — he smiled — "she cooks very well. Come."

Gratefully Phoebe took her place by the fire and accepted the noggin of water, the bannock, and the birchbark bowl full of stew from Shakoti'nisténha. Peter told her it was porcupine stew. The meat was as sweet as pork and as tender as the kernels of corn that added their own flavour to the rich gravy. Phoebe had an almost overwhelming urge to put her face down into the bowl and eat like the cat. But, as the others did, she dipped her fingers into the bowl for the pieces of meat and mopped up the gravy with the bannock. She gave the last of it to George, who had sat by her as she ate, stretching out his paw and crying angrily. The other three laughed.

It was only after she had mopped up the last of the gravy from her second portion of stew that Peter asked her why she was out in the woods alone. He sat with his back against a large birch tree, his legs stretched out in front of him. Moonlight gleamed on the white bark of the tree and on his black braided hair. He was cleaning his pipe with a twig, something Phoebe had seen him do a hundred times or more by her own fireside. It made her feel comfortable.

"Peter" — she inched herself a little closer and lowered her voice as though enemies lurked behind every tree — "I do not know that I should tell you. It is not mine to tell."

"Little Bird, I have not lived to be twenty years of age, nearly half of it in the white man's world, by casting words about as the milkweed casts seeds."

Phoebe was very still. Should she tell Peter about the message? She knew he would not divulge its contents because she knew his word was good. She knew, too, that the Mohawks fought as allies with the British and that Gideon's note had said to take the message to the Mohawk Elias Brant. But it seemed somehow like a betrayal to tell Gideon's story to anyone.

"I must tell you," said Peter, "that I knew

you had left your uncle's home. A relative of mine who had reason to be in Hanover saw you there. He ——"

"He was following me. I knew there was someone!"

"He sent me word, and we were watching for you, Little Bird. It is not wise for you to be alone in the woods. Not three days since there was a great battle south and west of here near the Hudson River at a place called Freeman's Farm. The British lost that battle — but that matters little to you. What matters is that now not only are the woods full of wild animals, they are full of soldiers, deserters from both armies, and not all good, kind men. A young girl alone is not safe. You have no one, and you have not even a firearm to protect you. I doubt you have as much as a hunting knife."

"I have a knife." Phoebe turned away and reached under her skirt to bring the wooden-handled paring knife from her pocket.

Peter looked at it, and then at her, in astonishment. "You...you mean to defend yourself against assault with that?"

Phoebe looked at the knife. Suddenly she felt ignorant and small. "I...I thought ——"

He did not let her finish. "Little Bird, it will not do. There are desperate men in these forests. Some are wounded, they are all, doubtless, hungry, and all have been without women for weeks. There cannot be one among them who would be stopped by your little kitchen knife."

Peter's mother spoke up. "Ro'nikonhri:io is right, daughter of my son's teacher. It is not good for you to be away from your home, out in these bad times, where you do not understand the ways of the forest. It is not good."

"We are none of us safe," said Peter. "My father was killed in July at the battle at Hubbardton, by Lake Bomaseen, across the mountains. My mother's brother has been scouting for the British in those hills along the Upper Connecticut River. When my mother and sister are safely in his care, I will join my brothers to fight with the British. Now, will you tell me what brings you out into this danger?"

Keeping Gideon's story to herself no longer seemed so important to Phoebe. Peter had been so concerned about her that he had spent precious time looking for her when his family needed him. And, too, he had made her see how much she needed his help. So, in as few words as possible, she told him about finding Gideon in her house in Hanover and everything that had happened afterwards.

She drew a deep breath. "So you see, Peter, I must do this for Gideon. You must see that."

"I do see, Little Bird, how you feel, but the danger is very great. Furthermore, you will not travel as swiftly as your cousin would have done, and you may not get this message to Fort Ticonderoga in time to be of use to General Powell. No, I think you must turn back."

Phoebe said nothing for a time. She had not considered that she might get Gideon's message to the fort too late. There was a sudden weight in her chest. But there were those Loyalist families needing help. She had to get word of them to the General.

"No, Peter, I must not turn back." She put her hand on his arm and looked intently into his face. "I must take Gideon's message to Fort Ticonderoga. My father was killed fighting for the rebels in Boston. Gideon was killed because he was a soldier for the King. I don't know which one of them was right, and I can't do anything for my father, but I can do this one thing, this one last thing, for Gideon and maybe save those poor families from what happened to Deborah Williams. I must try, Peter." She sat back and put her hands in her lap. "And I don't understand, Peter Sauk, why you care who wins this terrible war."

Peter drew long on his pipe, then blew out the smoke, all the time watching her gravely. "I think it will not matter to the Mohawk who wins this war. Whoever wins, the Mohawk will not win. But our greatest warrior, Thayendanegea, and his sister Konwatsi'tsiaiénni, who leads an important society of matrons of the Six Nations, both tell us it will be better if we stay with our old allies, the British. In return for our help, the British have promised to defend our land against encroaching settlers. I believe we have no choice but to trust them and, without our help, I do not think they can win this war. Konwatsi'tsiaiénni was wife to Sir William Johnson, the British agent in the Mohawk Valley, and she has power with the British. So has Thayendanegea. My chief has decided to follow their leadership. He has sent our warriors to fight as allies to the British general Guy Carleton in Montreal. I will follow my chief as I follow Thayendanegea, who was, like I, a student of Dr. Wheelock's, but it grieves me, Little Bird, to turn from the path of my old teacher, Jonathan Olcott, for I honoured him greatly." He reached out and touched Phoebe's hand. Neither of them said anything, but Phoebe felt that there was understanding between them.

Shakoti'nisténha stood up. "Now it is time to sleep. No more talk," she reproved Peter.

Phoebe was very tired. She settled for the night between Peter's mother and sister, wrapped in her shawl and her cloak, her feet warmed by the embers of the fire. Her last thoughts before she fell asleep were about Peter's mother and her kindness.

But her first thought on waking was that she could not let Peter Sauk, for all his kindness, tell

her what she should do. Then there was breakfast of corn-meal samp that tasted so like the
samp she had so often cooked over her own fire
at home that she felt a sharp stab of homesick-
ness. For one second she almost said to Peter
that she would go back to the Connecticut River
with him. And when he asked her if Uncle Josiah
and Aunt Rachael knew where she had gone,
she almost cried.

"N-no," she stammered, " I just came away."

"Did you not think they would worry?"

Phoebe didn't know what to say. With the
shock of Gideon's death, Anne's turning against
her in such fury, finding the message in the hollow tree, and at last making up her mind to carry
it for Gideon, not once had the thought entered
her mind that her uncle and aunt might worry.

"I will get word to them," said Peter, and
Phoebe knew he would no longer try to per-
suade her to go home.

"I must not tarry here. Nor can I take the
message to General Powell. My errand is too
pressing. The rebels do not deal kindly with their
Mohawk neighbours and I cannot risk the safety
of my mother and sister. And, Phoebe Olcott,
I will not carry you prisoner to the Robinson
family. While you are truly a gentle little grey
bird, I know you to be as stubborn as Ohkwá:ri,
the bear. I would need to watch your every move
and I have no time for that. So you must listen

closely to what I tell you, and frequently consult the map I will give you."

All the time he had been speaking to her, Peter had first peeled a deep section of bark from a large birch tree, and then drawn on it with a pencil he had on a cord around his neck.

He instructed her, pointing often to his map, to follow Kaniatarà:ken — in English, the White River, he said — beside which they were camped. He told her the river kept south of the high mountains, and so there was an ancient Abenaki path that followed it. He showed her where to turn south from the river when it turned north, and from there to keep to the lower hills. He indicated the old paths along the smaller waterways and the village of Rutland, where she would come upon the military road. Phoebe remembered the military road from the torn map Gideon had used to write his letter to Polly Grantham on.

"The military road will take you through settlements. Strangers are not made welcome in frontier communities these days. Furthermore, there are zealous rebels who actively hunt Loyalists to kill or imprison them, so you must not walk on the road. They will not stop to check if your father was indeed a rebel, and, what is more important, that message would betray you as a Loyalist. Stay in the forest, but always keep the road in view. When you come to the village of Shoreham, you leave the military road. Here, leading south, is an old Abenaki trail. Follow it to Shaw's Landing at the narrows of Lake Champlain, where you can see Fort Ticonderoga high above the shore on the New York side of the lake. Do not mistake it. After you leave the White River there are only brooks and small streams until you reach the lake. At the narrows the lake looks like a river. You will have to find a boatman to take you across the lake. You must be very careful!"

Phoebe nodded, concentrating intently on Peter's instructions. She was afraid to speak. The warning tone in Peter's voice and the careful outlining of the journey frightened her more than his talk of deserting soldiers had done.

Peter handed her the map. "If you mean to be as stubborn as I fear..." He paused. When Phoebe said nothing, he continued. "My mother and I have decided you must exchange clothes with Katsi'tsiénhawe. You are much of a size, I believe, so it will not be difficult. You will not be so noticeable in my sister's clothes; the danger may not be as great. And you may need to roost in trees." He grinned and Phoebe knew he was remembering her adventure the day before with the young bear. "There will be streams to leap," he went on. "You may find caves to sleep in, and all the ohkwa:ri you may meet may not be as timid as yesterday's cub. Your encumbering skirt will not serve as well as the *ionthsinohrókstha* and *akia:tawi* my sister wears. He turned to Katsi'tsiénhawe, who smiled hopefully back at him. "Katsi'tsiénhawe greatly admires your many-coloured coat. She would be happy to exchange it for her blanket."

Phoebe glanced down at her mother's tartan cloak wrapped around her. It was old, it had moth holes, its fur lining was worn to a smooth finish, but parting with it would be like parting for ever with all she held dear. She took a step back, her mouth opened to refuse to give up the cloak, but then she looked at Peter, at his sister, at his mother. How could she be so ungrateful? Katsi'tsiénhawe's father had died in the war, as hers had, and soon her brother was going to leave to fight in that war, and maybe die. And maybe someone she had loved had made her embroidered tunic. Swiftly, before she had time to reconsider, she unhooked the silver fastener at her neck, took the cloak from her shoulders, and thrust it into the girl's hands. Katsi'tsiénhawe smiled shyly at her and handed her the red blanket. Then Peter walked along the river to give the girls privacy and they exchanged the rest of their clothes. The only thing Phoebe did not give away was the pocket she had worn on the string around her waist under her skirt. She tucked it, with its message inside, into one sleeve of the tunic she put on.

How strange the leggings felt. The soft leather was like having another skin on her legs and she felt not quite dressed. The long tunic did not seem quite so strange, even though it, too, was deerskin. It was more like the blouses and shifts she was used to wearing, but warmer. And it was beautiful, with its intricate bead trimming around the neck opening, and its fringe on the shoulders and along the sleeves and the hem. She did not mind seeing her gown on Katsi'tsiénhawe, although it was a little like seeing herself in a looking-glass that was skewed. She and Katsi'tsiénhawe both smiled self-consciously when they looked at each other in their unaccustomed clothes. She minded, though, when the other girl stroked the tartan cloak admiringly — but saw too her small, sad frown when she herself fingered the supple skin of the tunic. She turned, relieved, when Peter's mother spoke to her. Shakoti'nisténha was holding out a bit of ground, parched white corn in a little birchbark wallet.

"If you find yourself by a stream where the fish will not come to you and the trees will not yield you their nuts, you have only to mix this with water to keep you from starving," said Peter.

"No." Phoebe shook her head vehemently. "No. You will need it yourselves."

"When we are feeling the pangs of hunger,

Little Bird, we will know that you are feeling them, too, but not one moment before us. And, soon, I fear, you will not be such a round little bird." He grinned ruefully.

There was a lump in Phoebe's throat as she accepted the corn from Peter's mother. It was easier, sometimes, she thought, to hold back tears of grief than those that came of unexpected kindness. She bowed to Peter's mother and sister. She bowed to Peter. Then she threw her arms around him and hugged him. He hugged her back.

With the wallet of dried corn stowed in her pocket together with the message for the General at Fort Ticonderoga, her map held tightly in her hand, Phoebe set off towards the west, along the old Indian path beside the White River. She liked the river. It wasn't as wide as the Connecticut, but it flowed as swiftly and splashed as exuberantly over the rocks in its path as did Trout Brook. There wasn't much wind, the day was bright and cold, the sky was blue, and the sun made ever-changing patterns of light and shadow on the moving water. It was the kind of day to raise the darkest spirits. She walked easily in Katsi'tsiénhawe's unconfining leggings.

She did not travel alone. She hadn't passed the first bend in the river when she heard a familiar meow at her heels, and there was George, weaving himself around her ankles, sniffing at the unfamiliar scent of Katsi'tsiénhawe's leggings. They were tramping along companionably, with George coming and going but never straying far, when Phoebe heard the sound of an animal snuffling somewhere near. She stopped walking and looked around her. A young black bear was scratching its back against a pine tree about two yards from where she stood. "Dear Father in heaven," she breathed, "another bear."

The bear looked up and saw her. It stopped scratching and ambled towards her. She backed away. Not George. George ran right up to the bear and rubbed himself against its legs.

"No, George! Oh no!" Phoebe cried. She closed her eyes. She couldn't rescue him, she couldn't run. She waited for his agonized scream. It didn't come. Slowly she opened her eyes. The bear was standing still, and George was rolling around at its feet, ecstatically. Realization hit. "You're not another bear," she said. "I know you. We spent all that time in the tree together." It occurred to her, then, that because this was the same bear and because it was young was no reason to ignore the fact that it was a bear, a bear that could be dangerous. Cautiously she began to back away again.

"Come on, George," she whispered, "Come on," but she didn't wait for him. She turned around and began walking, very slowly at first, then faster and faster until she was almost running. She heard grunting close behind her. She knew it was the bear. She stopped and turned. The bear stopped.

"Go away!" she gasped. She pointed back towards the pine tree with a shaking hand. The bear did not move.

"Please go away," Phoebe pleaded. Still the bear did not move. He looked at her expectantly.

"Please. I don't want you here. George," Phoebe begged, "will you please tell the bear to go away?" Suddenly it occurred to her that she was asking a cat to talk to a bear because the bear wouldn't pay any attention to her. Forgetting her fright and the need to be quiet and cautious in the forest, she laughed right out loud. It was the first time she had laughed, she realized, in a very long while.

At last she caught her breath. What did it matter if the bear wanted to follow along for a while. He did not seem to mean her harm and he was clearly company — if odd company — for George. Maybe he would scare off other big animals — and dangerous people, too. She decided, since they would be travelling together, she would have to give him a name. Because he made her think of an old woman in Orland Village, she called him Bartlett. "Mistress Bartlett always looks hopeful like you," she told him, "and she's bottom-heavy, too."

And so the long, difficult journey was

resumed. Phoebe grew braver with every passing day. She no longer jumped with terror every time she heard the whirring of owls' wings overhead or a partridge suddenly flew up in front of her. She walked carefully but briskly. There didn't seem to be much point in being especially quiet, not with a blundering young bear at her side and a complaining cat at her heels. And George did complain. He demanded to be carried when he got tired and he yowled when they would not stop for him to drink, or to stalk prey.

They spent one day scrambling up the side of a mountain, then sliding down its steep, rocky slope on the other side, other days slogging through swamps in the rain. They crossed streams and they crossed meadows. The snow that had been on the ground when Phoebe had left Orland Village had melted in a few warm days, but it was growing colder again and she could see snow on the higher hills. The days were shorter. There was ice edging the ponds and streams. The fish swam deeper and were harder to catch. There were fewer and fewer ducks and geese flying south, and almost no leaves on the elm, oak, and maple trees. Only the golden tamaracks still brightened the pine and cedar swamps and forests. Sometimes, Phoebe walked all day with Katsi'tsiénhawe's blanket around her against the wind and snow. And how glad she was of it at night. So were George and Bartlett. They curled up beside her, near the fire, and would not be budged. Bartlett stank. Phoebe tried to keep a space between them, but every time she pushed him away, he rolled over to be beside her again. Wherever they slept — by streams, protected from the wind by rocks or little hills, in mountainside caves — they slept in a tight ball of warmth, until Phoebe got so used to Bartlett's rough fur and rank bear smell she no longer minded either one.

Phoebe — and Bartlett — ate fish and what few huckleberries, blackberries, or raspberries could be found on bushes; they ate butternuts, hazelnuts, and hickory nuts from the ground under the trees, and whatever purslane, peppermint, chicory, or other edible plants had survived the frost in warm, sheltered places. George did his own hunting.

They saw no one. They followed the route Peter Sauk had laid out, keeping to the White River, then branching off to the southwest along the old trails by the brooks and smaller rivers through the deep valleys between the mountain ranges. Phoebe's heart was full of gratitude to Peter for his careful map. She knew she could never, ever, have made her way through the dense forests and around these great mountains without it. Finally she reached the military road, a rough road but wide enough, not only for marching soldiers but for wagons and carts. Carrying George much of the way, with Bartlett grunting and snuffling nervously beside her, Phoebe skirted the road and the settlements of Rutland, Pittsford, and Brandon but nearly went into Shoreham just because she so longed for the sight of another human being.

One cold evening spitting with the kind of thick, slushy rain that is almost snow, Phoebe camped early. For once she was planning to have a real supper. She had found a blackberry bush, hidden between a sumac and a blackthorn, amazingly untouched by birds or bears. She had gathered the berries quickly before Bartlett could eat them all, had held them in her tunic while she'd made a small leaf basket, then carried them in that.

Soon afterwards they had crossed a little stream. Phoebe had taken her vine and her hook and, at first try, caught a trout that was almost eight inches long. Holding it — and the berries — high over her head with one hand so that neither the cat nor the bear could get them, she was attempting to gather sticks for a fire with the other hand when Bartlett began to growl. She growled back at him. She had discovered that it always stopped him when she did that. She went on with her work. Then she heard voices approaching. She dropped the sticks. She dropped the fish. She dropped the berries.

She grabbed George and swung up in the nearest tree. Bartlett was right behind her.

Within minutes two men came into view. They had muskets over their shoulders and they were dressed in the fringed cloth shirts and deerskin leggings of rough woodsmen. Paralysed with fear, Phoebe peered down through the bare branches of the tree to watch them. They stopped directly below her. One of them took the pack from his back, and reached into it to bring out a dead duck. The other one bent over and picked up Phoebe's fish. He grunted. "Looks like someone's been here, Abel."

"Yup. And they ain't stayed long. What's more, they left us a trout. You git the fire a-goin', Jake, 'n' I'll pluck the duck. This 'n' that fish'll be a mighty-fine extry. I got a hunger on me says I could eat a whole hog." He hunkered down and started plucking the feathers from the duck.

His companion was not as easy in his mind. He prowled around, nosing behind bushes, walking a few feet this way, a few feet that. Once he looked up, but not straight up, and by some miracle the shadows of the surrounding trees, and the sleety rain, which had begun again, obscured the dark shapes of Bartlett, Phoebe, and George.

"I smell bear, Abel, I swear I do," he insisted.

"Wal, it wan't no bear what piled them sticks, 'n', what's more, no bear I ever heard tell of woulda left his fish a-lyin' around fer us to pick up. Come on, Jake, git the fire a-goin' afore these sticks is too wet to burn."

Up in the tree, George sniffed. Phoebe grabbed him and he bit her arm. She jumped. He wriggled free, fell, and landed on Bartlett. With a roar of terror, Bartlett fell off his branch and landed on the man called Jake.

With one powerful heave, Jake threw the bear from his back and took off. Swearing a long string of oaths, Abel grabbed his gun and tore after him. Bartlett huddled at the foot of the tree, whimpering. Phoebe scrambled down the tree trunk.

She ran and ran until her terror abated enough for her to stop to catch her breath and to think what to do. She knew only that she had gone in the direction opposite to the one those men had taken, but she had no idea what direction it was. George and Bartlett were nowhere in sight, the rain had definitely turned to snow and the night was very dark. She was lost. She tugged her blanket up over her head. She was afraid to move lest she head in the wrong direction, but she was so sure the two men were only over the next hill, ready to jump out at her, that she was afraid to stay where she was. So she set out, praying that an angel of God would protect her, lead her aright, and keep Bartlett and George safe.

The last part of her prayer was answered just before dawn. It had stopped snowing and she had sat down in the lee of a low hill to rest and fallen asleep. She woke when Bartlett rolled over to lie almost on top of her. She pulled herself up and looked around her. The sky was clear and pink with the dawning of a bright day, but, glad as she was to see her two companions, she was hungry, tired, footsore, and miserable. It was the first morning of the whole journey that she didn't bother to splash her face with cold water or rebraid her hair. She wished, with all her heart, that she had gone home to Orland Village with Peter Sauk and his mother and sister.

Bartlett found butternuts under the trees for himself. Phoebe had to settle for a bit of watercress from the edge of the stream. She drank a lot of water to keep from feeling the hunger too keenly. She resented Bartlett and George, too, for the nuts and for the unmistakable odour of fish they bore. "I expect you ate the duck, too," she said crossly.

She plodded along without offering a word to either animal, stopping only to check the trees for direction signs, then pushing one foot in front of the other up hill, down hill, over a stream, two streams, maybe three, until, bone-weary and discouraged, she slumped down with her back against a huge boulder on a hill that sloped down to a wide river. She put her head back and closed her eyes. She listened to the high-pitched *scree-scree* of the gulls, barely starting at the shotgun slap of a beaver's tail. The cat came and rubbed against her.

"Don't vex me, George. Go find yourself a fish in that river. I can smell the fish from here." She opened her eyes. Gulls! She was listening to gulls by a river. The river! After you leave the White River, there are only brooks and small streams until you reach the lake... Hadn't Peter said, Be careful — down where Lake Champlain narrows, it looks like a river — you may not know it at once for the lake?

Her heart began to pound. Under the afternoon sun, water gleamed through the branches of the hardwood trees. "Let it be the lake. Dear Father in heaven, let it be the lake," she whispered. Slowly she walked towards it through the trees, hardly noticing the bushes and saplings she pushed aside in her path. She came to the edge of the water. There, across its shining surface, high on a cliff, where Peter had said it would be, she could see the ramparts of a fort.

Below the cliff was a boat landing, but she could see no boats either there or on the water. Everything looked deserted. She looked around, feeling that, somehow, some means of getting across to the fort would present itself. And it did. Not three feet from where she stood, a rowboat, half buried by leaves and small tree boughs, was anchored to a willow sapling that hung over the water. Phoebe gazed down at it in wonder. She leaned over, lifted the boughs, and swept away the leaves. She touched one of the oarlocks.

"An angel is surely guarding over me," she breathed. "Gideon, I *will* get your message to your general at Fort Ticonderoga."

CHAPTER 7

There's Nobody There

"Here!" Phoebe heard a hoarse shout. "What're you doin' with our boat?" A man came barrelling down the slope at her. She turned to run but he was too quick for her. He grabbed her by the arm and she would have fallen if he hadn't had such a tight hold.

"Oh, please!" Desperately she tried to pull free. "I only meant to borrow the boat. I have to get across the lake to the fort. Please! I'll bring it back." She forced herself to look up at him, then the frantic beating of her heart slowed as she realized that her captor was a boy, probably not much older than she was. He was tall, as tall as a man, he had a man's deep voice, but he had a boy's angular thinness, and the face glaring down at her from under a coonskin cap was beardless.

The boy tightened his hold on her arm. She

winced. "I don't aim t'let go of you until I know what you're doin' here," he said. "Why d'you want to git to the fort? It ain't gonna do you no good on accounta there ain't a body over there."

Phoebe was stunned. "What do you mean there's nobody there? Where is General Powell? Where are the British soldiers? Oh, there must be someone there!"

At the mention of General Powell and the British soldiers, the boy loosened his grip. "Well, there ain't," he said, "not a livin' soul. They've gone, every man jack of 'em. How we're gonna lick the goddam rebels with General Burgoyne and the like in charge is a thing I sure can't figure. Our Gentleman Johnny Burgoyne's gone and pulled Powell and his soldiers out of Fort Ti with the same kind of good sense he had when he lost us them battles at Freeman's Farm and Bemis Heights over on the Hudson River; same as when he lost us the ones here at Bennington and Hubbardton. He just up and left you thievin', murderin' rebels to do whatever you dang well please."

"I am not a rebel! And I'm not a thief! Please, will you let go of me? I won't run, I promise, I won't, and I can't think with you holding me like this. Please, you're hurting me."

The boy gave Phoebe a long, suspicious look. Slowly he took his hand away. Backing up a step, rubbing her arm to get the blood running in it again, Phoebe tried to digest his news. What was she to do? If what the boy said was true, who could she give Gideon's coded message to? And who would help those Loyalist families?

"I didn't mean to hurt you." The boy shifted his weight from one long, skinny leg to the other. The anger had faded from his eyes, eyes that were a startling bright blue in a face that was otherwise very ordinary looking. He had a wide mouth and a blunt nose, and those eyes set in a square face almost completely covered with freckles. Tufts of reddish-blond hair poked out from under the fur cap pulled low over his forehead.

"Anyways" — he frowned at Phoebe — "you ain't said what you're doin' here dressed in them Indian clothes, tryin' to steal a boat to get to a place that's as cleaned out as a chicken coop after the fox has been. There ain't likely to be none of us Loyalists left in these parts, neither — we're all gone. So there's nought fer a spy to do."

"Gone? All the Loyalists are gone? Where?"

"I can't say fer all of us, but the rebels come to our place two nights since. Middle of the night. Neighbours, they was, and they booted us out of our beds and said we had to git. Tried to take me along with 'em to fight in their consarn army, but I got away and hid in the woods 'til last night. I snuck back to get our boat, and rowed up here to catch up with Ma 'n' the little ones. I ain't got time to stand here all day gabbin', but I ain't leavin' until I find out what you're up to." With an impatient gesture he pushed his cap back from his forehead, revealing the frayed edges of a dirty bandage.

"Oh, what happened to you?" Instinctively Phoebe stretched her hand towards him.

"Aw, I got into a tussle with the varmint who was fixin' to cart me off." He tugged the cap back down over his forehead. Unexpectedly he grinned. His whole face lit up, and Phoebe wondered, suddenly, why she had thought him so ordinary-looking. Then he frowned again. "I ain't settin' one foot afore the other until you tell me what you're doin' here," he said stubbornly.

Phoebe didn't know what to say. What could she tell him? She couldn't tell him about Gideon or trust him with either the coded message or the names of the Loyalist families. For all she knew he might be lying to her, *he* might be a rebel spy. "I'm on a mission," she said finally, "or I was on a mission — to Fort Ticonderoga — but, if it's true that there's nobody there, I don't know what I'm going to do."

He stared at her, not believing or not taking in what she had said, Phoebe wasn't sure which. Then he shrugged his shoulders resignedly, and looked up at the sky, where dark clouds were gathering in the east. "I got to head out," he said. "It looks like rain — or snow, more like — and I got to find Ma. She set out north for the Iroquois River up in Canaday. And, if I was you, I'd head right on back to where I come from."

Back to where I come from. Everything the boy had been saying suddenly struck Phoebe like a physical blow. The breath went out of her, her shoulders sagged. Back. Back over those mountains. She couldn't. And she knew, with a shiver of horror, that she could not go back to Orland Village. She had carried Gideon's message, had done the work of a Loyalist scout. These men who had hanged Gideon would hang her, too. She saw a long canoe gliding on the lake towards the south near the opposite shore and a flock of ducks fly into the air in alarm. They did not seem real. Nothing seemed real.

"You can't just stand there," the boy said impatiently. "There's wild animals hereabouts 'n' there's soldiers in the rebel fort up top of that mountain only a mile back. Get yourself on home. I'm settin' off to find Ma and Miz Anderson."

Anderson. Phoebe stiffened in surprise. Anderson was one of the names in Gideon's message. She knew those names by heart, she had read them over so often. Could this be the same family? "Are you related to the Andersons?" she asked. "I mean the family of Septimus Anderson who lives near Skenesborough, New York."

"Not me, I'm Jem Morrissay. Andersons live a couple of miles up the road from us."

Morrissay, another of the names. They must be the families on her list. And they were not safe. She had come too late, just as Peter Sauk had feared.

"Jem Morrissay," she began. She was going to ask about the Colliver family, but he interrupted her.

"See here, how do you know... Oh, Jehosaphat!" In one swift movement, he grabbed Phoebe by the arm and shoved her towards the boat.

She heard a low growl, and Bartlett emerged from the underbrush, his snout stained a deep red.

"He's bleeding," gasped Jem. "Sure as shootin' his ma's gonna be right behind him, set to kill. If you can run, you'd better start. COME ON!"

Phoebe yanked her arm free. She dropped to her knees beside the bear. "Bartlett, I forgot all about you, I'm sorry." She stroked his rough fur. "I'm sorry. Wherever did you find berries with enough juice for this much red?"

"Jehosaphat!" Jem's voice was shaking. "You must be addled!"

Phoebe looked up. "He won't hurt you and he has no mother. His name is Bartlett."

"Bartlett? Bartlett? Where'd he get a name

like that?" Jem's face was flushed with embarrassment.

"I gave him the name. He made me think of Old Mistress Bartlett back in Orland Village. You see, her hair is the colour of bear fur, and she eats as much as her pig, so she's big, not tall, mind, but, well, my cousin Gideon says three axe handles across the beam. I think maybe only one and a half, but she does look a bit like a bear."

Jem looked at Phoebe as if he really did think she was mad. "Where'd you get him?"

Phoebe stood up. Bartlett whined. She leaned down and stroked his head, again murmuring soft encouragements to him. She felt better. Bartlett's berry-stained snout and Jem Morrissay's discomfort at having been so scared seemed so ridiculous that they had restored her balance. "In a tree," she said. "I found him in a tree."

"Where'd you come from?"

"Over the mountains by the Connecticut River."

"You never did! A little gal like you, rigged out in squaw clothes? You and...and that bear to see a general at Fort Ti who ain't even there? I don't believe you." He crossed his arms and glowered at Phoebe.

"I didn't know he wasn't there."

"How come you wanted to see the General

anyways?" Jem seemed to have forgotten that he was in a hurry to find his mother.

"It was because of the mission to the General I was entrusted with," Phoebe answered stiffly.

"Well, there ain't a British general to see until you get to Fort St. John's, up on the Iroquois River, the one that runs north from the lake up to the St. Lawrence. That fort's near a hundred miles from here, in Canaday. And the forts south of here is all took by the rebels. I'm off now." He turned away, then, an instant later, he swung back. "And, if you're minded to get up to Fort St. John's, you can get yourself — and that bear — up there howsomever you come here. You ain't comin' along with me. I got enough to look after." He climbed purposefully up the slope to the path. When he reached it, he set off towards the north. He had only gone a few paces when he slowed, stopped, then turned around.

"I can't just leave you here, blast it! Come on. Ma'll know what to do with you. But God save you if you turn out to be a rebel spy." Suddenly he grabbed Phoebe's arm. "Don't say nothin'," he whispered; "there's a whole passel of men out there on the lake. They're paddlin' this way, and there's no sayin' who they are or what they're up to. Come on!"

Dragging Phoebe after him, Jem started along the path, crouching low and running as fast as he could, with Bartlett right behind.

Phoebe did not utter a sound, did not try to free herself, although her wrist, where Jem held her, was beginning to hurt — she was working too hard just to keep from hitting her head on low tree branches and stumbling on the rocks and roots in the narrow path.

When they had gone a good distance north of the men on the lake and Jem had slowed down, Phoebe pulled herself free of his grip. "Thank you," she said primly. "I can manage without your holding onto me."

"Don't you worry. I don't figure to look after you, and I'll tell you right out, I ain't takin' that bear to Canaday. No matter what you say, I ain't takin' no bear up to Canaday."

"You don't need to." Phoebe was equally indignant. "If you're going to Fort St. John's in Canada, march yourself right along. You don't need to look after me or the bear. We can find our own way, just as we've been doing for at least three weeks now." She meant it. At least, she meant to mean it. She was not willing to become indebted to this cross boy who distrusted her.

"Well, you can do as you please, but this ain't the best time in the world to be traipsin' through the woods on yer own." Jem turned his back to her and, as she'd bidden him, marched off.

Phoebe was tired and hungry and she had

never felt so alone in her life. Not when her father died, not when Gideon died and Anne turned on her. Not when she reached the source of Trout Brook and thought she was lost for ever. The only direction life had at this moment seemed to be to follow this irritating boy. And if she were to follow him to where his mother and the Anderson woman were, there might be comfort and kindness with them. And she had no will to start out again on her own. So she followed him. Bartlett followed her.

They hadn't gone more than a few yards when a dark shape leapt from a tree onto Phoebe's shoulder. Claws dug through her tunic into her skin. She jumped. And she screeched. Jem spun around.

"Where'd that cat come from?" he bellowed.

Phoebe looked nervously around to see if their noise had attracted attention. Jem lowered his voice to an enraged whisper. "I ain't takin' no cat. Ain't it enough you got that blasted bear? You didn't say there was a cat." He let out an exasperated sigh. "Where'd he come from?"

"From home. He followed me."

"He got a name, too?"

"His name is George."

"George? For George Washington, I guess."

"No, he's named for ——"

"I know, for some stupid-looking fella with red hair and a set of whiskers."

"No, it was more his ears and the way his eyes stare." Phoebe pulled George from her shoulders and shook him. "You scared me out of whatever wits I have, George. I thought you were a catamount." George jumped to the ground.

"You got any more family that come along over the mountains with you like Bartlett and George? Mebbe a nice friendly rattlesnake?" Without another word Jem started off again, walking at a furious pace.

"Jem Morrissay," Phoebe said timidly.

He didn't reply. He just walked faster, and Phoebe had to run to keep up with him.

"Jem Morrissay." Again.

He still did not reply.

"Jem Morrissay, you're going in the wrong direction. You're taking us east."

"I come the way the path come."

"It had a branch."

"Huh?"

"The path. It had a branch off to the east. That's the one we're on."

He looked at her suspiciously.

"Jem Morrissay, why would I mislead you? Look at the trees." She showed him where the moss grew and pointed at woodpecker holes that made almost straight lines, which meant east. Without a word of thanks, he retraced his steps to where the paths separated, and they started on the northward one again. Until they heard voices coming towards them. They got off the path then and hid in the thick bushes until the people had passed, two men and a woman talking in loud, cheerful voices about "the trouncing they'd given old Gentlemen Johnny and his redcoats at Saratoga and Freeman's Farm."

In about an hour, they reached the place near Chimney Point where the path crossed the military road. There they left the path and moved inland into the forest in order to avoid the road and the ruins of the old, burned-out French settlement that gave Chimney Point its name. "It's only that old chimney and a lot of rubble, but God knows who might be camped there," Jem said.

It was not really cold, despite the threatening snow, and Phoebe was not uncomfortable as she walked steadily and silently. She was glad the land near Lake Champlain had no high mountains. And she was glad, as she had been so often, of the deerskin leggings and tunic that did not catch on every bush and bramble she had to push from her. The way through the forest was dim. The pines and spruces cast thick shadows over the bare branches of the hardwood trees. The spicy scent of the evergreens was strong in the damp lakeside air. Small animals scurrying away from their scent and the thumping of their passing, Bartlett and George snuffling along behind her, and the harsh cries of the jays and the piping sounds of chickadees and kinglets announcing that strangers were on the way accompanied her thoughts.

She was trying to make some sense of all that had happened. From the moment Jem had said, "There's no one at the fort," the dispiriting thought had been creeping up on her that she had once again been stupid, really stupid. How could she have believed that, alone, without any knowledge of the war's battles and the movement of soldiers, she could carry out a soldier's mission? If only she had stayed in Orland Village! She knew that Anne's hysterics never lasted forever; she would have gotten over them. They could be comforting each other with the rest of the family in front of the warm fire in the kitchen. Instead, she was following a strange boy through the wilderness, a boy who, if he could be believed, was part of one of the families she had set out to save — too late. The realization of what she had thrown away for what she now saw as high folly sank into her as though she had swallowed a lead weight.

After they were sure they were well past the ruins at Chimney Point, Jem led the way back to the path along the lake, although he did have the grace to mumble that he didn't suppose he was "all that much of a guide." But, before they went on where the path led north, away from the shore, they slid down the slope to the lake for a drink. Gratefully Phoebe cupped her hands and drank until the water was dripping off her chin. Jem put his face right down into the water and sucked it up the way a horse does. He wiped his mouth with his hand and sat back on his heels. He watched Bartlett wade into the lake and George sniff at its shore. He looked at Phoebe, one eyebrow raised.

"You got a name?" he asked.

It seemed so long since anyone had said her name that Phoebe looked at him in surprise.

"You must have a name."

"Yes, I am Phoebe Olcott."

"From over the mountains."

"By the Connecticut River."

"That's a fair distance."

"Yes."

"Well, Mistress Phoebe Olcott from over the mountains, whatever brung you here, we gotta get on our way. But I'd sure admire not to be takin' that bear — nor the cat, neither."

"They'll follow."

"I reckon so. Let's go."

About an hour later, when the sky had darkened so much that Phoebe knew it must be late in the day, she heard the sound of voices in the distance ahead. Jem slowed. He motioned Phoebe to do the same. He pulled his hunting knife from its sheath, then, crouching low, looking to either side of him, he continued cautiously.

Phoebe was right behind him. As they proceeded, the voices grew louder, more distinct.

"I hear cows," said Jem. He straightened his pace and, in a few minutes, they reached the edge of a large clearing. Phoebe saw several open fires with people collected around them, and carts and two or three cows at one edge of the clearing.

"There they are," Jem said, "but there's sure a lot more of 'em than I figured. Come, I see Ma." He strode into the clearing. Phoebe followed nervously, suddenly not so sure of the kind reception she had anticipated.

A tall girl was standing by one of the fires about two feet away. She had her back to Phoebe, but something about the way she was standing, something about the set of her shoulders and her long light brown hair falling over her rose-coloured shawl made Phoebe's heart lurch.

"Anne?" she whispered. "Anne Robinson?"

The girl spun around. Her mouth fell open. Her eyes went wide. "Phoebe!" she cried. And slid to the ground in a faint.

CHAPTER 8

Anne

At the sound of Anne's cry, Aunt Rachael came running. At once, she was on the ground, with Anne's head in her lap, looking around wildly to see what had happened. She saw Phoebe. Her hand went to her throat. Her eyes widened. She half rose to her knees. Then her whole face lit up. At that moment a tall, stout woman appeared, carrying a pan full of water. She flung it into Anne's face.

Anne sputtered, and struggled to her feet with Aunt Rachael supporting her. A moment later she caught sight of Phoebe. "You're dead," she cried. "I know you're dead. We saw that squaw wearing your mother's cloak. We *saw* her!" Anne's voice began to rise to that hysterical note Phoebe knew so well.

Phoebe realized she had been clutching Jem Morrissay's arm and let it go quickly. She took a step forward. "It was Peter Sauk's sister. I gave it to her. I..." Her voiced trailed off. She was suddenly acutely uncomfortable. In the growing dark it seemed as though a hundred people had gathered around Anne. In the flickering light from the fires dotted around the clearing behind them, they looked menacing. "I...she... we exchanged our clothes. You see, I have her Mohawk ones." Nervously she gestured towards her tunic, and moved close to Jem.

Anne seemed not to hear her. Clinging to her mother, water still dripping down her face, she cried, "You're a ghost! I know you're a ghost! You've come to haunt me because I said those things to you when Gideon..." She began to cry piteously.

"Anne." Phoebe ran to put her arms around her weeping cousin. Anne shrieked at her touch and backed away. "Go away! GO AWAY!"

"For the sake of all that's holy, stop that caterwaulin'. It don't take but half an eye, and that one blind, to see this ain't no ghost." A short, stout man had come, elbowing people aside, pushing his way to the front of the crowd. He shook Anne's arm roughly.

Anne stopped crying. In the sudden silence a child's voice sang out, "That ain't no ghost, that ain't no ghost, that's my brother." A small girl detached herself from a red-haired woman standing just behind Rachael Robinson and threw herself at Jem. He scooped her up into his arms and he grinned at the red-haired woman. "I brung you some more company, Ma." He looked around at all the people. "Though I don't guess you was lookin' for it. She come from over the mountains, she says. Her name's Phoebe Olcott."

"She's dead! She's a ghost!" Anne's voice started to rise again.

"No, I am not," Phoebe said at the same moment that Aunt Rachael said, "That will do, daughter. You can see quite plainly that Phoebe is no ghost." She drew Phoebe into her arms and held her close. "Thanks be. Thanks be to Providence for your safe return to us. Later, when we have had supper, we will talk. Now, child, come with me. Come, Anne."

Phoebe turned to obey. The shock of seeing Anne and Aunt Rachael here was, if possible, greater than the shock she had had that morning when she'd found she could not give Gideon's message to the General at Fort Ticonderoga. Her mind was spinning. What had happened? How had they come here, almost to the shore of Lake Champlain? Why? Even in the gloom she could see how worn her aunt looked and that her usually fastidious appearance was marred by a soiled gown. But she seemed so much the same kind, quiet, capable person she had always been that Phoebe felt comforted.

"No." Anne stepped in front of her mother. She would not look at Phoebe. Her voice shook. "I wish she were dead. She should be dead. It's her fault we're all out here in the wilderness with no place to go. It's her fault Gideon died. She's a traitor — didn't her father fight for the rebels in Boston? Didn't she run away right after Gideon was killed? What is she doing out in the woods alone? Alone! Phoebe Olcott is too scared of everything that moves to come out in the wilds alone. I don't believe she's alone. There's someone else, others like her, waiting to murder all of us. She's a traitor like her father! Make her tell!"

For a moment the silence was so intense that the sharp howl of a wolf in the near distance was like an echo of Anne's last words. It was too dark now to see faces clearly, but, by what light there was, Phoebe could see the people, shuffling, moving. She could feel them coming slowly towards her. She could hear their low muttering. "No," she cried, "it isn't true. Aunt Rachael, I am not! Jem?"

He backed away from her. "You sure musta been laughin' at me talkin' about the things you rebels done to us," he said bitterly. The angry whispering from the crowd was louder. A man stepped forward, a stick in his hand. Phoebe felt as though her heart would stop beating. She grew icy cold.

"No!" She swallowed hard. "Anne? Aunt

Rachael?" She stopped, her mouth too dry to form words.

Rachael came swiftly to her side and put her arm around her. She turned and faced the crowd. "We are all in this same sorry state," she said. "It is no time to be turning on our own. Don't we all know how that feels? Phoebe is no traitor. I know she is not." She looked around at the other people, her arm tightened protectively around Phoebe's shoulders. "Come, we must get you something to eat and a place to sleep. No one will hurt you."

"Mother!"

"Anne, we will have no more of your hysteria tonight."

Anne said no more, but the look she gave Phoebe made Phoebe slip closer to her aunt, and all night that look would give her nightmares. She let herself be led through the hostile crowd to the fire beside which Jed, Noah, and their father were all sound asleep. Still shaken, she was standing, gazing bemusedly down on all their faces, when someone cried, "Bear!" She looked up to see Bartlett lumbering towards her across the clearing as fast as he could, with George trotting along beside him. She heard a child scream. She saw men priming their muskets. She ran.

"Don't!" she cried. "He's an orphan. He won't hurt anyone. Please, oh, please don't."

She threw herself to the ground beside the bear. She was no longer afraid for herself; all she could think was that no one was going to kill her bear.

Amazingly Jem stepped forward. "Let the bear be," he said gruffly. "Go ahead and shoot that wingein' cat if you wants to, though," he muttered, as he took his little sister's hand and walked away. The crowd fell apart into tired families huddled by fires kept burning high enough all night to hold the wolves and cata-mounts at bay. But not the nightmares.

CHAPTER 9

Camp

Phoebe woke just before sun-up the next morning. She sat up and looked around her. She had been sleeping on a bed of pine needles under an enormous pine tree. It stretched its thick green branches over her, keeping away both the wind and the snow that had sprinkled the ground in the clearing beyond. Between the stumps, at a little distance from one another, small knots of people slept around the embers of camp-fires. Aunt Rachael, Uncle Josiah, and the boys were huddled together under a quilt a foot or two from where she sat. Anne was wrapped in her cloak with her back to them.

Even in the dim light Phoebe could see that there were not nearly as many people as there had seemed to be the night before. She counted seven camp-fires, including the Robinsons', and there looked to be no more than twenty-five or thirty people.

She shuddered, feeling again the terror she had felt when those people had moved slowly towards her in the night's half dark. They all hate me, she thought. They think I'm a rebel and a spy. I must leave, I mustn't stay with them. Near her, Rachael stirred in her sleep. As dim as the light was, her features were clearly discernible and they looked so careworn, so sad, even in sleep, that Phoebe knew she could not leave, not without a word, not again.

"How they must be worrying about you," Peter Sauk had said. And last night, before she could roll herself in Katsi'tsiénhawe's blanket beside Bartlett and George, Rachael had pulled her into her arms.

"What Anne said is true," she had whispered. "We all thought you were dead," and Rachael Robinson, who had not wept for Phoebe's father or for Gideon, not where anyone could see her, had had a catch in her voice and, even more astonishing, had kissed Phoebe on her cheek. Aunt Rachael was so reserved that the only time Phoebe could remember her actually offering physical signs of affection was when they had stood together by Gideon's coffin and she had put her arm around her.

Anne had refused to talk to Phoebe or to look at her. When her mother gave Phoebe a dish of the boiled beans she had cooked for the family earlier, Anne had walked away and not returned until she had lain down to sleep — at a conspicuous distance. But, despite the fatigue that wearied them both, Phoebe and Rachael had talked long into the night. Phoebe had realized, as soon as she had settled safely by her aunt's camp-fire, that she must tell about coming upon Gideon in Hanover and about the message in the hollow tree that had sent her across Vermont's Green Mountains to Fort Ticonderoga. When she had come to the end of her story, Rachael had said nothing for such a long time that Phoebe had feared she would say nothing, ever, about what she had been told. It was not so. In a low voice, heavy with tears, Rachael had said, "There was never any dissuading Gideon from whatever he determined to do, not from the moment he was born. How well I remember him — he was only three then — stubbornly refusing to eat your mother's fine gingerbread that he loved when we wouldn't give any to our old beagle because sweets made him vomit. But Gideon managed, when no one observed, to feed his portion to the dog, who was soon violently ill. What was important to Gideon he would do, and he never stopped to consider the consequences. He would go off into the woods for his plants no matter what else needed his attention. He would go off to fight for the King against your uncle's deepest convictions — and mine. And he would come home to see his Polly, no matter how risky it was. I should have known, I suppose I did know, when he went off to war, that he would never come home to us."

She had taken Phoebe's hand. "I know that God means us not to succumb to life's trials, Phoebe, but sometimes life's trials seem more than a body can bear. The loss of that dear boy…" Rachael's voice had become so low Phoebe had hardly been able to hear her. But the voice had strengthened and there had been a note of humour in it. "He was most certainly a wilful soul, our Gideon, and" — she had squeezed Phoebe's hand — "so are you. I cannot fathom what was in your mind to set you out over the mountains alone, without confiding in a soul about what you had found or what you meant to do, you who were always so much a stay-by-the-fire child. Why, Phoebe? Why did you not tell us?"

Holding tight to Rachael's hand, Phoebe had gazed intently into her face, its pained expression evident in the light of the fire. Haltingly, she had confessed to Rachael that she had been sure, from the moment she had agreed to take Gideon's letter to Polly Grantham, that she should not have done it.

"If I had not taken that letter, he would not have gone near the village; he would be alive and you would not be out here in the cold forest.

Anne was right, even though she didn't know why. It's all my fault, all of it."

Phoebe had been trembling when she said those words, in part from the misery she felt at what she had done, in part from the relief of having told Aunt Rachael. Rachael had wrapped her arms around Phoebe and held her close.

"You must not believe that. It is not true, Phoebe. Gideon ought not to have been in Hanover for you to find him there. He ought not to have written to ask Polly Grantham to meet him. He ought not to have asked you to deliver his letter. You are not guilty of those acts. You ought not to have taken it upon yourself to deliver the message you found in the tree, but you were grieving, and Anne ought not to have blamed you for what happened, but she, too, was grieving."

"I know, Aunt Rachael. I know how Anne is. Only," Phoebe had said in a small voice, "I thought she would get over it and she hasn't — she still believes it was my fault. And she believes that I am a rebel because Papa was."

Rachael had sighed. "Try to be patient with Anne, Phoebe. Do you know, she is so like your mother. Your mother, my sister, was as pretty as Anne — that same fair hair and those same violet eyes, and, I fear, that same coquettish manner. And your mother, too, you may as well know, was inclined to think of herself before she thought of others, but she was a loving soul and so is Anne. Anne loved her brother and, although you may doubt it just now, she loves you. I think that you and Gideon were anchors for Anne's mercurial nature. She has not said so, but I think it grieved her sorely that Gideon did not find a way to see her when he stole into the village to see Polly. And then you left us in the night, without a word."

Phoebe understood jealousy. She remembered how she had felt when Gideon had called Polly the dearest girl in all the world. But, as for Anne grieving over her departure, she did not quite believe that, not with Anne still calling her a traitor and refusing to speak to her. But she had said nothing. Instead she had taken from her sleeve the worn linen pocket containing the silk-covered paper that had brought her all this distance from home. She and Rachael had crouched by the fire, their heads close, and in the flickering light they had puzzled over the coded words directed to the General at Fort Ticonderoga, and together read the message about the Loyalist families from New York.

"But these are the people we came upon this very day," Rachael had exclaimed, "Peggy Morrissay and her small daughter — the boy James you came with is her son — Abigail Colliver and her two little ones, and Bertha Anderson and her three. Just today. How strange!"

She had told Phoebe, then, how Elihu Pickens and his Committee of Public Safety had come to their door the night after they had buried Gideon — late, after they had all gone to bed.

"I feared they would come. So I had put by provisions and blankets, a few spare clothes, our family bible, a cooking pot and dishes. I packed them all in the big carved chest that was my mother's — your grandmother's. We had our ox and cart, and they let us take one cow. Your uncle Josiah has a cousin living just outside Bennington on this side of the mountains, so we went south along the Connecticut River to Fort Dummer, then west to Bennington along the waterways through the woods. We learned quickly to keep from the roads. That's when we saw Peter Sauk's sister wearing your cloak. We were too frightened to go near them and, I suppose, Peter did not know who we were." Rachael shook her head sadly. "I wish Peter could have told you about me. He meant to try to see you," said Phoebe. "People were not kind. It took two weeks. But Cousin Robinson was not pleased to see us. Being a God-fearing man and strong in the church" — Aunt Rachael had permitted herself a wry smile — "he took us in, but he said it would be impossible for us to stay. He saw to it that we were provisioned, but he kept the cow in payment. So we came north from there, keeping out of the way of villages, keeping to the woods west of the high mountains. A few times we met people. Some were kind, even offering shelter in a barn or old cabin, but most turned their heads from us, and more than once people jeered and called us names. A gang of rowdies threw mud and stones at us — we were frightened. Even Jed and Noah were subdued! But the heart of Providence was with us, for the noise of their shouting startled a family of deer from the bushes and the villains went after them. Not far from the battlefield at Hubbardton, we came upon a skeleton with enough scraps of scarlet cloth and a silver gorget to identify it as having been a British officer. We hadn't a shovel with which to give it Christian burial, but your uncle read the service over it from the Book of Common Prayer and we prayed for its poor soul.

"Two days ago, by the Lemon Fair River south of here, we met Charity Yardley, her son, and her father-in-law, Thomas and Margery Bother and their boy, and Joseph and Lucy Heaton — all Vermonters from near Bennington who'd suffered the same fate as we. We decided to join forces, hoping that the old adage 'safety in numbers' would prove true. Only this morning, we came upon the refugees from New York. They had suffered much. Two of the women have husbands fighting with Loyalist regiments. The third's husband has been dragged off to prison. One of their brothers was hanged before their very eyes when he would not divulge the whereabouts of his landlord to a troop of rebel soldiers, and a neighbour was tarred and feathered."

"Aunt Rachael" — Phoebe was close to tears — "I should have been with you. I could have helped you, I could have helped with the boys. It must have been so hard!"

"What is done, is done," said Rachael firmly. "Now, Phoebe, we have talked enough, and wept enough, for one weary night. Let us have a prayer and then we must sleep." Together they bowed their heads while Rachael thanked God for Phoebe's return to the family, asked His blessing on their journey, and prayed for Phoebe's father, for Gideon, and for the others who had died in the war.

Phoebe had not slept at once. She had lain beside the sleeping bear and cat, listening to the wind in the high branches of the pine tree, to the long cry of a wolf, the bark of a fox, a screech owl's insistent hooting, thinking about all she and Rachael had said to each other. Now, in the morning, she was thinking again about all the Robinson family had suffered. She was not entirely reassured by Rachael's telling her that none of what had happened was her fault. She knew she would carry to her grave, even if she lived to be a hundred, the conviction that if she had not taken Gideon's letter to Polly Grantham he might not have had to die, and that Aunt Rachael, Uncle Josiah, Anne, and the children might still be living at home in Orland Village. Anne's hysterical words still ran over and over in her head, the words she had screamed when they stood by Gideon's body hanging from the Liberty Tree, the words she had screamed only last night: "It's your fault! You're one of them! You should be dead!"

One of them. And those other people, those Loyalist families she had failed to save, and the Vermonters, too, thought she was a rebel, a spy. If they really thought she was a spy, a girl who wasn't quite fifteen years old, mightn't they hang her as quickly and without question as those men had hanged Gideon? She swallowed back a sudden lump of fear and clenched her fists. How they hated rebels for what they had done. How could they not? But she was not a rebel — or a Loyalist either.

I don't know what I am, she thought unhappily.

She made herself take a slow, deep breath and, when she had calmed herself a little, she sat back against the tree and surveyed her surroundings. In the morning light she could see that the clearing was small, not more than fifty yards across, an open space between a brook and a spruce-and-cedar swamp to the east, a low hill rising protectively to the south, and the woods through which she and Jem Morrissay had come to the west and north. Filled with those great tree stumps, the clearing was obviously man-made, probably by someone meaning to settle, Phoebe decided, but likely discouraged because it was so swampy.

At the hill edge of the clearing was a narrow path leading north. Beside the path there were four ox carts. Near them, four oxen and two cows stood impassively on the frozen ground. Phoebe looked down where Bartlett and George slept by her side. There was comfort in the quiet animals, so unconscious of the trouble people made for themselves.

In the soft dawn light, the jagged stumps were blurred at their edges. The thin snow and the frost on the tall grass, and the dry leaves on the sumac and honeysuckle by the verge of the swamp, glistened as the first rays of the sun touched them. Nearby a woodpecker began his rattling peck-peck-peck. Holding herself motion-less, Phoebe looked for him in the tamarack tree by Aunt Rachael's head. She couldn't see him, but she did notice that the tamarack had lost its golden needles. Winter was not far off.

A frail-looking old man got up from his fire on the other side of the clearing and hobbled into the woods. Bartlett groaned and rolled over onto Phoebe's feet. George rose, yawned, stretched, glared at Bartlett, and walked off. Phoebe needed to go off into the woods to pee, too. And wash. She yearned for Aunt Rachael's copper tub in front of the kitchen fire, although, she realized, with some surprise, that she had gotten so used to living in Katsi'tsiénhawe's leggings and tunic that she hardly felt dirty any more.

Other people began to stir. A big woman covered by an enormous green surtout stood up over near the ox carts, the woman who had thrown the water over Anne. She jammed a broad-brimmed felt hat onto her head over the bedraggled mob-cap she was wearing and at the same time began at the top of her voice to order the small children stirring by the ashes of her fire: "Johnny, go fetch a jug of water. Betsy, let that child be. What are you a-bawlin' about, Tibby? I declare you was give to me jest to see if I was good enough to be made into a saint." It was not only a loud voice, it was a rough voice. It woke everyone in camp. One of the children began to cry. The woman yanked her to her feet. She looked over at Phoebe.

"Here, you, bear girl," she shouted, "come and give a hand with this kid. You might better make yourself handy. We got no time for slackards on this here jauntin' party."

Phoebe was too surprised to refuse. She took a quick look at where Jed and Noah still slept, then hurried across the ground to the woman's side.

"Take her," the woman commanded. "Just lift her up 'n' cart her off. I ain't got time to be watchin' what them kids is up to all the time. Spy or no spy, I don't figger you'll harm the little 'uns. Now you, Betsy, you mind." She reached down and pulled another little girl from where she'd been hiding in the folds of the big, green surtout. Phoebe took the wailing child by the hand.

Not ceasing to wail for an instant, the child darted a ferocious glance at Phoebe and snatched her hand back. Phoebe picked her up and she began to writhe and to wail louder. But Phoebe was bigger, and the weeks in the woods had made her not only thin, but strong. She carried the child to where her kicks would not land on someone's head. "You'll do, now," she said, and set the child on her feet, but she kept a firm grip on her hand. Tibby — that was what her mother had called her — was small and probably not more than three or four years old, but she was wiry and she was determined to get away. Phoebe held tight, relieved that, in her struggle, Tibby had stopped crying.

"Come. We'll go find water and wash the tears from your face."

"Don't 'ont to."

"Do you want to go back and fight with your sister?"

"Ain't my sister."

"Well, do you want to go fight with her anyway?" Phoebe was losing patience.

"Ain't goin'."

At that moment Jed and Noah Robinson came charging towards Phoebe, their arms outstretched. They grabbed her, each by a leg, all but throwing her to the ground.

"Phoebe!" shouted Noah, "You don't know where we've been! You don't ——"

"It's like Robinson Crusoe in your book, Phoebe," Jed's excited words drowned out his brother. "We was ——"

"We was riding in the cart and then we walked and walked and we ——"

"We saw Papa's cousin. He ——"

"He was a sour old man and ——"

"But we didn't stay there because we liked the cart better, but Anne cried and cried and ——"

"And I'm glad to see you and we are all together." Phoebe barely managed to talk above them. She got down on her knees and hugged them both.

"Yes, but we thought you was dead. Papa said a lot of prayers, and Mama said you were with Gideon, and Anne said she ——"

"And Phoebe, Phoebe, Gideon got ha ——"

"I know, Jeddy, I know."

"Mine," said Tibby. She gave the boys a hard shove, one and then the other. "Mine," she repeated. She wrapped her arms and legs around Phoebe. The boys thought this was a good game and began to climb on Phoebe's back.

"Boys!" she tried to make her voice stern, but she was too glad to see them, and she laughed. She reached behind her to pry them loose. Finally she found the word that worked. "Breakfast," she said, and the boys slid off her back. She stood up. Tibby was not so easily shaken loose. She locked her legs around Phoebe's ankles, her arms around her knees.

"Have done!" Phoebe demanded, but Tibby was so small and so spindly, her arms and legs no thicker than the rungs of Aunt Rachael's keeping-room chairs. Dressed in an old grey linsey-woolsey skirt that had obviously belonged to a much bigger child, a man's weskit that almost came down to her ankles, and a tattered shirt, she was so pathetic Phoebe could not be too impatient with her.

"You are a bindweed, Tibby, to wind your-self about my ankles. How can I walk?" Tibby stared at her, unblinking.

Noah took Phoebe's hand possessively. "This is *our* cousin," he declared. With his other hand he tried to pull Tibby away, just as Bartlett came and shoved his cold black snout between Tibby and Phoebe's legs. Tibby shrieked. Frantically she tried to climb up Phoebe's legs. Phoebe lifted her into her arms.

"He won't hurt you," she soothed. "It's Bartlett. Go along, Bartlett." She gave him an impatient shove. "Go find George."

Bartlett paid no attention. He rubbed happily back and forth against her legs. Tibby was whimpering now, and Jed and Noah backed away nervously — but not far. They began to jog slowly around Phoebe and Tibby, coming closer to the bear at each turn. Two other boys had left their own camp-fires and watched, at a safe distance. Phoebe recognized one of them as Tibby's brother, Johnny. In this fashion they all progressed towards the fire, where Aunt Rachael was bent over a big pot, cooking breakfast. People everywhere were stirring up fires. The scent of wood smoke, boiling fish, and dandelion-root coffee filled the chilly air.

There was a sudden commotion over at the edge of the woods by the carts. Someone cried shrilly, "Oh, God in heaven, whatever am I to do now?"

Aunt Rachael dropped the ladle into her cooking pot and ran. With Tibby still clinging like a burr, Phoebe ran too. A small circle of people had already formed around an old man lying on the ground. His eyes were closed. A boy was sprawled over him, a crutch held tightly in one hand. The other crutch lay broken on the ground, beside them. A woman with thin grey hair hanging loose around her anguished face was standing by them. She was wringing her hands, moaning, "What am I to do? What am I to do?" over and over again.

A red-haired woman whom Phoebe recognized as Jem Morrissay's mother was on her knees, lifting the boy. As Aunt Rachael moved in to help, bending over the old man, she glanced around the circle quickly and saw Phoebe.

"Here, Phoebe," she said, "you take the boy."

Phoebe looked from Aunt Rachael to the child in her arms. "You have to get down," she told Tibby.

"Ain't." Tibby sniffed.

There was no time to be gentle. Phoebe wrenched the arms from around her neck. She held the surprised child by her waist and, nose to nose, glared into her eyes. "You get down and you stand here, still as a tree." She plunked Tibby down onto the ground, and the child stood there, unmoving, and did not make a sound.

In three steps Phoebe was beside the boy. She put her arm out for him, and he took it and let her lead him away across the clearing to the pine tree where she had spent the night. "You can sit here on my blanket," she offered.

He gave her a swift, distrustful glance and looked away.

"Do...do you think I mean to harm you?"

She felt the sting of tears behind her eyes. Even this child in pain distrusted her.

"It isn't that. It's my grandpa." The boy gulped. Phoebe put her hand out to touch his thin shoulder. He flung it off. He propped himself against the tree and, under the guise of straightening his breeches, began to rub his weak leg.

"Jonah! Jonah! How come you was a-lyin' on top of yer grandfer?" Tibby had not stayed where Phoebe had stood her for more than a minute. Her eyes were bright with excitement.

"How come you got to ask questions?" The boy turned back to Phoebe. "Please...?"

"But why was you?" Tibby danced up and down in front of him.

"Scat, you ugly little toad," he muttered, all the while surreptitiously rubbing his leg.

Phoebe watched the boy anxiously. She saw that, while both his legs were very thin, the right one was also twisted. She could see, too, that his face, under the shaggy black hair, was as grey as his grandfather's. She got down on her knees to look at his leg, although she didn't have the first idea what to look for.

He shifted it away. "Don't mind it," he mumbled. "Please. Grandpa." He couldn't say any more, but the agony in his eyes said it for him.

"I'll find out how he is." Phoebe got to her feet. "Wait here."

Jonah's grandfather was sitting up, leaning against one of the carts. His face was still drained of colour, his breathing heavy, but he was struggling to get up while Aunt Rachael, Jem's mother, and Tibby's mother tried to get him to drink some fish broth. The grey-haired woman who had been moaning and wringing her hands was still lamenting. "Oh, how could God have visited this woe on a poor widow? Thrown out into the cold wilderness with only a crippled son and an aged father-in-law to protect me, and now the old man is sick." Her voice rose. "Oh, dear God, how am I to manage?" She looked around her as if to discover someone to be responsible. Something in her pinched, discontented face told Phoebe that this woman always meant someone else to be responsible for what happened to her.

"There now, Charity Yardley." Jem's mother patted the distraught woman's hand, her own cheerful, round face creased in a sympathetic frown. "He's comin' along right smart."

"Oh, dear God, all the way from Bennington I knew, I just knew this would happen. I told him to stay back, he would have one of his spells, I knew he would. They wouldn't have troubled a feeble old man like him."

"Like as not the old man's paid his way lookin' after the kid," a voice muttered behind Phoebe. She recognized Jem Morrissay's deep voice. She wanted to turn, to say something to him, but she remembered the disgusted look he had given her the night before, after Anne had told everyone about her father being a rebel, and she didn't want to see that look on his face again.

"See here, woman, we got no time for such carryin' on. Stiffen up!" Tibby's large mother pushed both Rachael and Mistress Morrissay aside with a sweep of an arm. She stood in front of Charity Yardley, her hands on her hips.

"You can count on Bertha Anderson to give a body what for," Jem Morrissay said with a chuckle in Phoebe's ear.

Encouraged by that chuckle, Phoebe turned her head to smile back at him, but as she caught his eye he frowned and shouldered past her to help his mother with Jonah's grandfather. She felt as though she had been slapped. Jem's eyes had darkened with scorn. He still doubted her, still believed she had lied to him.

She started after him, then halted abruptly. There was no time for talk. There was Jonah. She ran back across the clearing to reassure the thin little boy, still propped against the pine tree, craning his neck in an effort to catch sight of his grandfather. Tibby was with him. So were Jed, Noah, and the two other small boys she had seen before the accident.

"Phoebe! Phoebe! You got George, you got George!" Jed was doing his best to climb up into the pine tree where George was perched, his tail swinging back and forth ominously.

"You'd best leave him, Jeddy. Jonah, your grandfather is all right. Mistress Morrissay and my aunt Rachael are looking after him. I collect you may be hurt worse than he is. I think someone had better look at your leg. My uncle Josiah has a little knowledge of medicine."

"There's no need." Jonah flushed. "I'll be right enough."

"But not right enough for walking this morning."

"No, Miss." He paused then went on in a low voice, "and I don't rightly know what Ma's going to say, either."

Phoebe thought about Mistress Yardley and said nothing. She did not know what to do for Jonah. She knew to use puff-ball spores for wounds, feverfew for fevers, jewel weed for ulcers, sweet flag for coughs and the like, but she could not cure his distress. She did not know what to do for herself either. It had seemed simple that moment by Lake Champlain when she had decided to follow Jem, to find his mother and Mistress Anderson. Now she would go with them, and with her aunt and uncle and her cousins, to the British Fort St. John's in Canada. She would deliver Gideon's message there. Even though it was too late to save the Andersons and Morrissays and Collivers, it might not be too late to deliver the coded message to General Powell, or to whoever was in charge at Fort St. John's. She would not break faith with Gideon.

And in Canada she would be safe from the kind of people who had tortured and murdered their neighbours, who so cruelly uprooted families, who had hanged Gideon. But last night. Last night! These people, these refugees who had been treated so badly by the rebels, had looked at her as though they wanted to hang her. How could she travel to Canada with them? Jem had been right when he'd said she must be addled — addled with grief and the stubborn need to deliver Gideon's message! But if she wanted to reach this fort, even though it might prove as unpromising as Ticonderoga, she had no choice but to travel with people who considered her an enemy.

Not all of them thought she was an enemy, not Aunt Rachael or Uncle Josiah or Jed or Noah. Maybe not Tibby's mother. And here was this bony, black-haired boy with his large, fierce dark eyes. He couldn't be more than nine or ten years old. He was hurt, crippled, his mother had said, and she did not want to look after him. But who would look after him? Would he quietly fall by the wayside and die when no one was paying him any attention? Could she leave him to that fate?

"Jonah," she said, "do you think you might

be able to walk if you were to use your crutch for your good leg and lean on me for your poor one — until the poor one is a bit better and your other crutch is mended? You might keep pace with everyone, then, mightn't you?"

"No, he mightn't!" cried Tibby, "No, he mightn't!"

"Why ever not?"

"Can't lean on you. You gots me to look after."

"No, I haven't. You have your mother to look after you."

"Ain't my mother. I'm a orphant. Pa got strung up 'n' Ma died in the fire. Miz Anderson took me up. Me 'n' Betsy Parker a-cause her pa's off in the war 'n' her ma's dead, too."

Phoebe sat down. She looked at the hurt, angry bit of a human being standing before her, fists clenched, wispy hair hanging around her thin face, pale eyes full of tears she would not shed.

"I am an orphan, too, Tibby. So I'd be glad to have you come along with me when we start walking."

CHAPTER 10

On the Move

Aunt Rachael was more than willing to share the family's breakfast of beans and cornmeal samp with Jonah and Tibby. Not so Jed and Noah. They were happy enough to have Jonah by their fire but objected loudly — and in unison — that "that little girl should go be with her own mama." And Anne — Anne walked away and refused to eat breakfast "with the traitor clothed like a squaw." Phoebe was desolate, not only because Anne despised her but because of how she looked. Anne, who had always managed a bit of lace on her white kerchief, a bit of bright ribbon for her hair, had no kerchief tucked into the neck of her blouse; her gown was dirty and there were tears in it. And Anne's hair, which had always been freshly washed though she had to help herself to the water heated for the laundry to do it, now hung in limp, dirty hanks, and there was no ribbon.

Phoebe looked towards the carts, where her cousin stood facing away from everyone, her back hunched miserably. In that one moment she couldn't help but think that Anne despised herself, too. The moment passed, but it left a kinder feeling towards her cousin, a feeling of sympathy she hadn't been able to manage the night before when Rachael had pleaded for it. She turned back to her aunt and uncle and the boys in a better mood. Uncle Josiah had returned from his morning wash in the brook. He smiled vaguely at Phoebe, but did not seem to recognize her. With a pang of horror, she understood what Aunt Rachael had meant when she'd said Uncle Josiah was "badly shaken" by what had happened. He had retreated into himself, where he could not be reached.

She wanted to comfort him, but she couldn't think how. What she could do, if she meant to make herself useful, to become someone to be trusted, was look after Tibby and Jonah along with Jed and Noah. She left Bartlett and George with the children and went to see Bertha Anderson. She offered to keep Tibby by her throughout the journey to Fort St. John's.

"Well, I declare I don't mind if you do." The big woman's face eased into an expression that was almost a smile. "Here, then, you'll need her duds, such as they are, and I expect I'll need to give you a bit of vittles so's the mite can eat. Mind, it's fer Tibby Thayer. I ain't supplyin' the what-fers for that Yardley lad I see you took on. Them Green Mountain folk can look after their own."

As she talked, Bertha Anderson rummaged among the bundles in her ox cart and came up with a small shawl-wrapped parcel, and a tin bucket into which she put a few handfuls of corn-meal. "There. Now you passel that out good 'n' careful on accounta it's all I got to give you. And, if you're some kind of rebel spy, which I suspicion you ain't on account of your auntie bein' such a good woman, and you causes harm to that mite, may God Almighty see you gets what's comin' to you. I got no special love fer that bothersome Tibby Thayer, it's true, but her ma 'n' pa was God-fearin' folk, rest their souls, and I don't want to see her bad done by."

Phoebe mumbled a thank you, took Tibby's bundle and the tin bucket, and hurried away before Bertha Anderson could give her the other little girl, whose name she thought she remembered as Betsy. It's a whole village full of names to remember, she thought as she went to find Mistress Yardley.

Charity Yardley, without a word, extracted from the belongings in her cart a pair of breeches, a shirt, one thin wool blanket, and a faded red

Monmouth cap. "And he'll have to make do with the stockings he has because the old man needs the spare pair." She sniffed. "Oh, I am sore beset."

Phoebe waited for her to ask how Jonah was, meaning to tell her the boy was not really injured but that he needed to eat, but his mother turned away, intent on straightening the bundles in her cart, and she did not offer any food. Phoebe was so angry that Jonah's mother should care so little for him that she was determined she would not ask for any.

"We'll manage without her," she muttered to herself as she marched away. "What a horrid woman! What a jest her name is!"

She had just sent the two boys to find their mothers, pulled both Jed and Noah from Bartlett's back, and given Jonah his spare clothes, explaining to him that she would get his broken crutch later, when a soft voice beside her said, "Forgive me for troubling you. I am Lucy Heaton, and Joseph, my husband, bade me inform everybody that we're preparing to move soon."

Lucy Heaton was a small, neat woman with mouse-grey hair tucked under a grey bonnet. She had a grey knitted shawl pinned tightly over a patched grey gown. Phoebe thought of a big-eyed deer mouse she had surprised once in the kitchen dresser at Aunt Rachael's. And Mistress

Heaton's voice, she thought, was just the sort of soft, quiet voice a deer mouse would have. It sounded furry.

"We have only to figure out which way to go," said the furry voice. There was a note of humour in it that Phoebe understood better after she had seen who Lucy Heaton's husband was.

Joseph Heaton was one of the most self-important people she had ever met. He was a short, stout man with a big, jowly face, the man who had pushed his way to the front of the crowd to stop Anne's cries the evening before. His grey hair was hidden, all but its braided queue, by a large black cocked hat. He had leather breeches, and a grubby vest with a dark flowered pattern on it, a shirt with torn ruffles, and a dirty white linen neckerchief. He's as pleased with himself as Elihu Pickens, thought Phoebe. I hope he is not as mean.

Phoebe, Jonah, Tibby, Jed and Noah (who had made a grudging peace with Tibby), along with everyone else in camp, had gathered near the path by the four carts. Joseph Heaton was standing a little apart, at the front of the assemblage. Clearly he had undertaken the role of leader. "Without so much as a by-your-leave," Jem grumbled to his mother. He was standing on the other side of Aunt Rachael with his sister Jeannie on his shoulders. Phoebe heard him plainly and she bit her lip to keep from smiling. Although they had spent only one day together, and in spite of his painful hostility, Jem seemed like someone she'd known for a long time, and his quick temper made her want to laugh.

Joseph Heaton heard him, too, and glared in his direction.

"As we need to move on from here, and as my party got started on this here exodus with a Injun guide — though the varmint up and left us two days since — I got me a good idea of how to git on with it. But if there's any a you got a better idea" — he glared at Jem again — "I'll be plum pleased to hear about it."

People looked at each other questioningly. Phoebe knew that the Morrissays, the Andersons, and the Collivers had all come up from New York only two days before, and not with any knowledge of how to reach Fort St. John's. The others were all Vermonters, Green Mountain people, but neither had they any knowledge of the more northern parts of this republic. And none of them knew the geography of Canada. They only knew that the river — the one Jem called the Iroquois River but Rachael had told Phoebe was also called the Richelieu — flowed north from Lake Champlain into Canada. And they were almost a hundred miles from its source at the top of Lake Champlain, so Jem had said back where they had met. Her thoughts were interrupted by hearing Jem say her name. She looked at him, startled.

"Phoebe Olcott's got notions about finding direction." He shifted uncomfortably and did not look at her.

Joseph Heaton looked at Phoebe. "Wal" — he looked around slowly at everyone else — "I wouldn't want no rebel spy leadin' me to Canaday. I can see it sits well enough with some of you" — he looked from Mistress Anderson to Mistress Yardley — "to keep this suspicious person in our amongst, but I ain't so easy bamboozled 'n' I aim to keep my eye strict upon her." He glowered at Jem.

Jem's mouth was clamped shut. From where she stood, Phoebe could not see his eyes, but she knew they'd be cold and hard. She could guess how it must have galled him to suggest to Joseph Heaton that she knew how to figure out direction, and to have to listen to that tiresome man do his best to humiliate him. Then she realized something else from what was being said. She understood that these people — including Jem — *were* going to allow her to travel with them to Fort St. John's. Suddenly they all looked more like friends.

The result of Joseph Heaton's certainty that he knew which way to go was that, with much bullying and blustering on his part, the children were herded into the carts, the fires quenched, the oxen hitched, the cows slapped on their rumps to get them going, and the company moved off west towards Chimney Point on Lake Champlain the way she and Jem had come, the start of the military road back to the east. Phoebe was scared to tell Joseph Heaton this, but she was more scared when she thought about heading back towards that road, towards rebel settlements or maybe companies of rebel soldiers.

"Do you think, girl," Master Heaton sneered, "that I don't know north from west, or where there's like to be danger?" All the same, he stopped and conferred with Jem and Thomas Bother, "jest to satisfy the whiners." Jem, who had paid close attention to Phoebe's lesson the day before in spite of himself, looked for the clues the birds and the moss gave, then realized he was looking towards where he and Phoebe had come into the clearing the evening before. And the company set out once more — to the north.

As they travelled, the cat stayed close to Jonah. In fact, George, who had never shown any affection to anyone, not even to Phoebe, had taken one look at Jonah Yardley, rubbed up against his good leg, and purred loudly. What's more, he slept curled up against Jonah every night. Bartlett stayed near Phoebe most nights, but he worried her by disappearing for hours during the day, longer hours and more frequently than he had on the journey through the mountains from the east. His presence had made the refugees nervous until they saw how he would roll over for the children and let them ride on his back, then they were even grateful to him. It wasn't long before everyone began to take him as much for granted as they did George.

What an ill-assorted company they were, the twenty-three Loyalist refugees. The Yardleys had been well-off shopkeepers in Boston when Charity's husband had died after being shot by a rebel mob in the first days of the war. She and Aaron, her father-in-law, and Jonah had gone to relatives in western Massachusetts, but the relatives had been, like the Robinson relatives, too frightened to let them stay. More generous than the Robinson relatives, they had given the Yardleys a cart, an ox, a cow, and provisions that they hoped would keep them warm and fed until they reached safety in Canada.

The Yardleys had come upon the Heatons and the Bothers north of Bennington, where both those families had been farmers. Thomas Bother was, like Phoebe's uncle Josiah, a peace-loving man. He came of Quaker people and had been unwilling to go to war, so he and his wife, Margery, and their eighteen-month-old son, Zeke, had had to leave their farm and all but a few bundles of belongings, and head north. An Abenaki friend of Thomas's father had agreed to guide the party, but Joseph Heaton had treated him so badly he had quietly taken off the second night out.

And then there were the refugees from New York, the three families Gideon's message had named. They had all come from just beyond Skenesborough, near Wood Creek, below Lake Champlain. The Andersons had owned a mill, but the other two families were farmers. Peggy Morrissay's husband, Charles, was fighting in a Loyalist regiment. Abigail Colliver did not know whether her husband, Jethro, was dead or imprisoned. He'd simply disappeared one day. Bertha Anderson had the same conviction about her husband, Septimus, although he, like Charles Morrissay, had left to be a soldier.

Back in Hanover, Phoebe had heard about the feuds between the people from New York, the "Yorkers," and Vermont's Green Mountain people, how they had never gotten along well because the governors of New York and New Hampshire had fought for so many years over that mountainous land that lay between them. While there had never been major battles, there had been skirmishes. Settlers had been run off the land they'd been granted by their province by gangs from the other province, houses had been burned down, people had been beaten.

While there had been no actual killing, there were hard feelings. Now, even though the refugee band held common cause, they did not really trust one another. So the families were more than willing to blame one another for whatever went wrong, and after only a week of travelling together, frightened, heartsick, cold, never certain of enough to eat, they were an unhappy lot. By the end of the first week, they had travelled no more than twelve miles, more often through treacherous swamp, dense spruce and hemlock woods, often up hills so steep that the oxen could not pull the heavy carts and goods had to be unloaded and carried. It had snowed and snowed and, for the last two days, there had been such high winds they had been forced to stay camped in the shelter of a pine woods.

On the third morning everyone felt better when the sun rose in a clear sky and the temperature had warmed. Joseph Heaton had just barked out the order to "git a-goin' now!" when three rebel soldiers burst into the camp. They were dressed in ragged breeches and homespun hunting shirts. One had stockings and shoes, the other two had rags wrapped around their legs, and one had rags for shoes as well. The only way anyone could know they were soldiers — or rebels — was that the youngest, boldest one taunted them, "Come along, you Tory cowards!

George Washington's fighting sojers is needin' a helpin' hand."

At the first sound of the soldiers' shouts, Jem Morrissay and Thomas Bother ducked behind the carts. Phoebe saw Jem pull his knife from its sheath, and Thomas had his musket at the ready. By the time the soldiers were upon them, Jem and Thomas were nowhere to be seen.

One soldier grabbed Jed Robinson and five-year-old Sam Colliver and held them at bayonet point while the other two rummaged through the carts. While the refugees watched helplessly, the men took a blanket, a side of salt pork, and a pair of shoes from the Heatons. They took one of Charity Yardley's cows and a flitch of bacon. They took flour and a quilt from Bertha Anderson — she told Aunt Rachael later than it was the one her grandmother had brought from England. She shook her fist at the rebels, but the young, brash one gave her a shove, then knocked her down with the butt of his musket.

"Here, you old sow," he jeered, "we ain't took it all, we only borrowed the loan of one of your cows. And you won't be needin' this here quilt — you got lots of fat to keep you warm. Now you jest give our love to old King George when you sees 'im."

Laughing uproariously, the soldiers tramped off. The sound of the bawling cow seemed to go on for ever. For a while Sam and Jed clung to their mothers, too frightened to make a sound. Even Tibby Thayer said nothing. Jem Morrissay and Thomas Bother reappeared. Thomas took one anxious look at his wife. Jem was tight-lipped and looked at no one. Joseph Heaton began, in a loud voice, to rebuke them, but six or seven voices instantly silenced him. They all knew three armed soldiers could have over-powered two young men before any one of them could reach a musket, tied them up, and marched them off to fight in the rebel army, or "hanged them for traitors," said Margery Bother, tear-fully clinging to her husband. Phoebe glanced quickly at Jem and shuddered.

For a day or so there were fewer harsh words, fewer disagreements about sharing provisions. Then, only a few days later, a pair of bedraggled British soldiers limped into their camp. There was no doubting that they were British. Dirty, sweat- and blood-stained though they were, the redcoat uniforms were unmistakable.

"To be sure, we have stumbled on a party of his majesty's loyal friends," the one said with an accent that made it immediately clear he was from across the sea.

The relief the refugees felt was short-lived. "What news is there of the war?" Jem asked impatiently.

"Not good news for us." The soldier grimaced ruefully. "Burgoyne lost his campaign on the Hudson River, and we've been in retreat ever since. Your Americans from the captured Loyalist regiments are up at Fort St. John's under convention not to fight — that means they can't go into battle, but they're bloody well free to lay about the fort. We regulars from over the bloody sea were taken prisoner; only some of us managed to escape. We're making our way to headquarters in Montreal as best we can. Now, if you will be so kind" — he made a deep bow to Joseph Heaton — "we are in desperate need of sustenance. I feel sure you will not begrudge two of his majesty's regular troopers a few necessaries."

"You can't take our supplies!" cried Bertha Anderson.

"Now see here —" Joseph Heaton began, but when the soldier pointed his gun at him, Master Heaton backed off.

Then, while his mate kept watch, his gun at the ready, and while Master Heaton sputtered indignantly, and the rest watched, tense and silent, the soldier took a ham from the Yardleys' cart, a sack of corn meal from the Heatons', and a sack of flour from the Robinsons'. He searched the Andersons' and Collivers' possessions, but when he found mostly children's blankets and shirts, he shrugged. "Not much use for these, or this" — he snorted, holding up Betsy Parker's penny wooden doll.

He caught sight of Anne half hidden behind Jem. He swaggered over to her and pulled her towards him. He grinned and bowed. "Jack Turner, at your service, ma'am." He took her by the shoulders and kissed her soundly on her mouth. Someone gasped. Anne's mother stepped forward, and Jem moved towards the soldier. Anne just stared at him. He laughed and bowed again, swung the sack of corn meal over one shoulder, tucked the ham under the other arm, and marched off whistling "The Dashing White Sergeant." The other soldier lowered his gun, picked up the sack of flour, and followed his mate into the woods.

"Deserters." Joseph Heaton spat after them — once they were well out of earshot. "On their way to Montreal! A likely yarn! On their way to hide out 'til the war's over is more like." He swore roundly, his jowls quivering with rage.

"Only deserters would behave like that." Charity Yardly sniffed at Anne and went to pull together what was left in her cart.

Aunt Rachael had her arms around Anne for comfort, but Phoebe had seen the flush of pleasure that had brightened Anne's cheeks. She couldn't help hoping the soldier's kiss would soften Anne's coldness. It did not soften her coldness, but it did return her a little to her old self. She began to pay attention to how she looked. She found a bit of a ribbon to tie back her hair, she found a kerchief for her dress. Complaining loudly, she washed, as the others did, by breaking the ice in ponds or putting her face into the fast-running brooks. As she always had, she managed to avoid all but the easiest chores. And she began to flirt with Jem. Phoebe's charitable feelings towards her cousin suffered a serious setback when she noticed Anne's flirtations. Why doesn't she go looking for kisses from Thomas Bother? she thought peevishly. But then, glancing over at the gentle farmer with his baby son in his arms, she was ashamed of herself for having so monstrous a thought.

The others were certainly not as cheered by the visit from the British soldiers as Anne was. Wearily they trudged on. Now and then they would come across an old trail that would make an easier passage, but they were always on the watch for spies, scouts, deserting soldiers, and Indians. Every single stranger in their path became an instant threat. The story of Jane McRea, the beautiful Loyalist girl who, only a few months earlier, had been caught in a dispute between two parties of Iroquois scouts, murdered, and scalped, had brought old fears about hostile Iroquois into their hearts. The experiences they had had with their own lifelong neighbours–turned–vicious enemies were fresh in all their memories and, when they got lost once and found themselves near a small forest settlement, they had slogged on all night to get a distance from it.

They all kept their muskets primed in case of enemies and in the hope of finding game. Phoebe had no gun, but she had more than once fired Gideon's old Brown Bess, so she shared the watch with Rachael. Anne would have nothing to do with the gun, and, despite their clamourings, Rachael would not let the boys near the musket. Every night Jem and Thomas and old Aaron Yardley set snares made of vines. The old man insisted that, though he might not be as strong as he had once been, he hadn't forgotten all his boyhood skills. Every morning they broke the ice on a brook or waded into a river to fish for trout or perch. Some days they were lucky and there were fish, or their guns would bring down a partridge, a turkey, or even a deer. Some mornings a porcupine or rabbit would be found caught in the snare. Now and then there were bushes with a few dry berries or chokeberries the bears or the birds had missed, but there were only ever enough to add a bit of flavour to the ever-thinning corn-meal samp.

Whoever had corn meal shared with those who hadn't, although Joseph Heaton complained loudly that he saw no reason to "fill in for the improvidence of others," especially since he had lost his salt pork to "those dad-blasted rebels and a sack of his meal to" — and he glared at Anne — "those foreign deserters you took such a shine to." Charity Yardley insisted that she had scarcely enough to keep her own, much less her father-in-law's body and soul together. When Peggy Morrissay pointed out to her that Phoebe Olcott, who had nothing of her own, was looking after Charity's son Jonah, Charity reluctantly dipped into her sack for a portion of meal. She was rigid with anger when old Master Yardley piped up that they could easily share the ham the soldiers hadn't taken and some of their flour. It turned out, to the outrage of many, that provisions were in good supply in the Yardley cart.

Still, none of it lasted long with twenty-four people to feed, and soon there was so little that, on poor hunting days, children could be heard all over camp, whimpering in their sleep from hunger.

Then, the Andersons' cart broke an axle and foundered in a brook at the foot of a cliff, and the company came to a halt. And that was where Jem's sister Jeannie came down with measles.

CHAPTER II

Axle-Broke Brook

The morning the axle broke on the Andersons' cart, Joseph Heaton told his wife, Lucy, loud enough for everyone to hear, that he wasn't going to "wait up for no passel of Yorkers and strangers just on accounta they didn't have the know-how to keep themselves goin'. Nor I ain't a-gonna set around waitin' for their kids to die of measles." And with no more of a farewell than that, the Heatons started off across the brook, their cart creaking under its load of food, farm implements, and the scholarly books Joseph had inherited from his grandfather but could not read. They didn't get as far as the other bank of the brook. The axle broke on their cart in a hole almost as deep as the one the Andersons had foundered in.

Phoebe told the children the name of the brook should be Axle-Broke Brook and made a rhyme of it. At once Tibby began tramping around the campground, chanting, "Axle-Broke Brook, Axle-Broke Brook, if you don't b'lieve it, you gotta come look."

Joseph Heaton snarled at Tibby and cast murderous looks at Phoebe, but there was no stopping Tibby, and soon all the children had picked up the chant, even Jeannie Morrissay, shivering with fever, wrapped in her mother's cloak, until there wasn't an adult who wasn't longing to duck them all in Axle-Broke Brook. At one point Jem threw down his end of the board he and Tom were trying to slide under Heatons' cart in the freezing brook and marched over to where Phoebe was keeping the children busy gathering firewood. Nose to nose, he glared into her eyes. "If you can't shut them up with that Axle-Broke Brook, I ain't gonna jest duck you in it, I'm gonna drown you!"

Phoebe jumped out of his way, but she smiled. A wary friendship had developed between the two of them. Jem had never said anything about Anne's accusations or about Phoebe's father, but it was hard to be not speaking, always angry, as they trudged through the deep woods, up and down the never-ending hills, camping every night in the freezing November air with the mournful sounds of wolves in the near distance, and the rustling of myriad small wild animals close by. So they had made a kind of peace. And now, on the bank of Axel-Broke Brook, she threatened, "I will sing you into the song." He only grunted, but she saw that one corner of his mouth turned up.

While the carts were being made ready to move again, Thomas and Margery Bother decided to go on ahead.

"I'm right sorry," Thomas told everyone. "I know you got a use for more'n one stout younger feller" — he looked apologetically at Jem — "but what with the baby due to be born in a few weeks and winter comin' on so fast, we're powerful keen on gettin' to Fort St. John's."

The Bothers left with Zeke in Tom's arms, Margery in tears. Hers was not the only sad face in the gathering that watched them go. But there was little time for the sadness of goodbyes. By the time the damaged carts were repaired, Betsy Parker, Jed and Noah Robinson, and Sammy Colliver had all come down with measles.

The brook beside which the refugees were camped, and which never lost the name Axel-Broke Brook, flowed north between a high clay cliff and a low wooded hill. At the spot where the Abenaki trail crossed it, the brook curled sharply around a bend in the cliff, leaving a broad margin of flat gravelly bank on either side. There were big willows and poplars along the banks, but they offered little protection from the November winds that whistled and moaned down the watery path, a wild echo to the fevered moans of the sick children. The little fires, clustered there between the hillside forest and the ice-covered brook, seemed like no security at all from the dangers of the wild.

The children were too ill to be moved, and even Joseph Heaton did not leave, although he said every day that he was going to and he complained loudly about the "dad-blasted Yorkers bringing their filthy diseases into Yankee lands." But he actually took his axe from his cart and bent his back to the work of lopping branches from the brookside willows and the pines from the woods to make rough tree-bough shelters against the bone-chilling cold and the worst of the wind and snow. Nothing could keep out the mournful cries of the wolves, and the growling and the snarling of the wolverines and the wild cats, nor the glowing eyes at the edge of the camp on dark nights, which only the carefully tended fires kept at bay.

Lucy Yardley wrung her hands constantly and whined that she would "surely die in this God-forsaken wilderness." Anne told her mother she was sure to have measles, though she had had them and recovered years before. While Jonah kept her fire going, it was Phoebe who sat up most nights cradling the children, fetching them water, and feeding them spoons full of the precious soup she had made from corn meal, fish, and the bits of ham the others brought her.

"I'll see you get help with the vittles and somethin' better to cook with than that old tin bucket of Bertha Anderson's." Abigail Colliver was as good as her word. She cajoled Charity Yardley into giving up one of her three cooking pots, and Phoebe felt well provisioned. Cooking pot! With the cooking pot she felt she had a real place in the camp, and she looked after the children with the same practical determination with which she had once looked after her father, had sorted Gideon's forest gleanings, had set out to complete Gideon's mission. She took Jed and Noah from Aunt Rachael because, she argued, "they might as well be fretful here beside me with the others."

Measles, even in well-ordered homes in towns and cities where there were licensed doctors, killed hundreds of people every year. Phoebe had survived them at the age of four when her mother and her infant brother had died. Now, out in the woods, without even a quack healer in their midst, the refugees were terrified. They gathered every morning and every evening to pray for the recovery of the sick children and that no more of them would succumb to the disease.

One evening, a day or so after the company had made their camp by the brook, Jem came by

Phoebe's fire with a couple of rabbits over one shoulder. "Here, you, Jonah. You handy with a knife?"

Jonah looked up from feeding twigs to the fire. "I guess so."

"Come along then. I could use a hand skinnin' these. For your pains you can bring back a hunk or two for your cookin' pot. Unless Phoebe needs you." He glanced in her direction and raised an eyebrow.

"I don't." She was so hungry at the thought of stewed rabbit she couldn't say another word.

Jem was back the next morning — he had been lucky with his snares again, and held a porcupine by its hind legs. "I got us a nice fat quill pig," he said cheerfully. "If I burn off its quills 'n' skin it, will you cut it up? Half's for Master Yardley, here, and half for you and Mistress Colliver. Ma's still got rabbit from last night, and old Heaton's shot hisself a partridge." So Phoebe, Jonah, and Tibby ate bits of boiled porcupine while the sick children drank the broth.

Aunt Rachael, Abigail Colliver, and Jem's mother, Peggy Morrissay, took turns nursing the children through the worst nights. Jonah's grandfather, who hadn't had another weak spell since that first one, came often to tell the children stories of his boyhood sailing out of Boston on the big ships. Most evenings Jem would bring some of whatever his gun, his snare, or his fishing rod had caught. Some evenings there was nothing, but he came anyway, bringing his sister Jeannie to sit by the fire, listen to old Aaron Yardley's tales, and drink the tea he made for them from the frozen mint or cress he found under the snow by the water's edge.

Gradually Betsy, Jeannie, the Robinson boys, and Sam Colliver recovered from the measles, and Tibby and Arnie Colliver and Johnny Anderson came down with them. Arnie was happy as long as he could lie with his head on Bartlett's flank. Tibby was sicker than all the others and much more demanding. Night and day she clung to Phoebe like a burr to a blanket, crying out in terror whenever Phoebe left her for a moment. Time and again Phoebe found herself grateful that Jonah had had the measles years earlier, because he not only kept the fire going, he fetched water from the brook, stirred whatever was in the pot, and, with the help of his grandfather, kept the convalescing children entertained.

Jem began to refer to Phoebe's campsite as her family. Sometimes he would sit by the fire and talk after the children had gone to sleep and Jonah's grandfather had settled down by his own fire. One evening he told Phoebe about growing up on the farm south of Wood Creek in New York. "It wan't like this, not all thick woods," he said. "When Pa bought the farm, it was cleared, all fifty acres. We had a white frame house 'n' a big barn. By the time we got kicked off our place, we had fifty head of cattle, a good team of Clydes, 'n' a whole passel of chickens 'n' ducks 'n' geese." Jem's tone was bitter. "When the war come on, Pa went off to fight in the Royal Yorkers. I was set to go off with him 'n' then he said, 'Jem, you can't come. I can't leave easy without I know you're here lookin' after things.' And then we was kicked off the farm by those thievin' Sons of Liberty. And they took everythin' but a couple of cookin' pots 'n' a handful of clothes 'n' vittles. They even took Pa's fiddle!" Jem's voice broke. "And how that burns! Oh, Jehosaphat, that burns! Pa's fiddle. When I think of that louse-covered, ham-fisted, no-good Gabe Jenkins scrapin' away at Pa's fiddle ——" He broke off. Even in the dim fire-light, Phoebe could see the anger on his face. She put out her hand, but drew it back, thinking he wouldn't want her sympathy. But he surprised her.

"Aw, I guess we all got the same troubles 'n' I never had to come all the way over the mountain like you did. Did you have a farm over there?"

Jem's telling her about his life seemed like a gift to Phoebe, so she told him about her loving but absent-minded, scholarly father and growing up by the college in Hanover. She started to talk about Anne and the friendship they had once had, but Anne and Anne's rejection of her were too present and she couldn't. She found, though, that, in the dark, with only the firelight to illumine their faces, she could talk about Gideon — not about his death, never that, but she could talk about those days when, looking back, it seemed as though the sun was always scattering its light through the thick leaves, Gideon always bending over his plants, smiling up at her. She talked about listening to her father and his students discussing ideas until the light of dawn would show through the cabin windows. And in a very low voice she told him about her father believing so completely in what he called "the Patriot Cause," and marching off to be killed for it.

"And you?" asked Jem. "What do you believe?"

Phoebe couldn't lie. She wanted to. She wanted to tell him that she believed with him that the rebels were wrong. But she couldn't. Her father's words about justice and freedom had been so passionate.

"I don't know," she said unhappily. "I don't know what I believe."

"But fer some reason you ain't talkin' about," he said after a long silence, "you up 'n' come over those high mountains all by your lone self."

"I wasn't alone." Phoebe grinned. "I had Bartlett and George, and we didn't climb to the tops of those mountains, we went around and through the valleys." Then, she told him about the afternoon in the tree with the cat and the bear. Jem laughed and his laughter woke Tibby and Sam, and Phoebe had to tell it again. When she'd finished they all looked over to where Bartlett slept with Arnie Colliver. But Bartlett wasn't there.

"Gone again," whispered Tibby around her bad throat.

"Again," echoed Phoebe. "It's true, he does go more and more." She felt suddenly guilty that she hadn't been paying more attention to Bartlett.

"Well," Jem said dryly, "mebbe you got enough to do without havin' to stop 'n' think what some bear is up to all the time."

"But it's Bartlett and...and you can laugh if you care to, Jem, but Bartlett's been a better friend to me than anyone in this entire world — except for Gideon, and...and Peter Sauk."

Jem's eyebrows shot up as they did when something surprised him. He gave a short, uncomfortable laugh. "I guess I done you no favour when I brung you to my ma."

"Jem, your mother is nice."

"That's so 'n' so are..." Jem stood up. He shifted from one foot to the other. He pulled his cap off and scratched his head. He seemed to want to say something, but, instead, he picked up a stick from the pile, threw it into the fire, watched while it sent sparks up into the dark night. "Leastways you've give up sayin' my whole name all the time. You sayin' just 'Jem' sounds a might friendlier." Without another word he walked off.

Phoebe stared into the dark night where he had gone. For a moment she had been sure he was going to say that she was nice too, and she was almost embarrassed by how happy that made her.

What happiness lingered in Phoebe's heart left her the next afternoon. She had gone along the brook with a bark bucket she had borrowed from Jem's mother. She had taken a few of those minutes when Aaron Yardley was telling the children stories to get away to wash herself. It was a cold day but clear and bright, and she had found a little rapids about a quarter of a mile around the bend in the brook and the ice wasn't thick. She had plunged her face into the rushing current, scrubbed it and her hands with sand, and then made a fresh braid of the thick, dirty tangle that her hair had become.

Feeling quite cheerful about the world, she started back along the gravelly bank, carrying the bucket full of water, humming to herself. She heard voices, Jem's and Anne's. She heard

Anne say her name. She dodged behind a large rock, until they would pass by. They didn't. They stopped only a few feet from where she crouched.

"How can you be friends with her," Anne was saying, "playing nursemaid to all those children so that people will forget she is not to be trusted? Well, I will not forget. Not ever. I declare I never did trust her."

"But ain't she your cousin? Wan't you friends?"

"Did she tell you that? No. No, we were not friends, not ever. How could you think that? I felt sorry for her. Poor, plain little Phoebe, as plump as a partridge and twice as timid. That's what my brother Gideon always said but he was kind to her. If he could only know...."

"Well, she don't seem so timid to me. She come all the way over the mountains on her own."

"It was because of Gideon!" Anne's voice rose. "She ran away after he was hanged. She knew we'd find out it was her doing."

"Your brother was hanged? She didn't tell me that."

"Yes, he was, and it was Phoebe's doing. She's a rebel, I tell you. I don't care what my mother says, Phoebe tells lies. Her father was a rebel. *He* got himself killed at that battle in Boston, so she was waiting, she was just waiting for her chance to make us suffer. It is her fault we were hounded from our home to skulk through this horrid wilderness like hunted animals. It is all her fault and I hate her!"

Jem mumbled something. Phoebe heard their footsteps move off on the rough ice and gravel. She crouched there, motionless, thoroughly miserable. Lies. They were not her lies. She stood up, blinking back tears, and stepped out from behind the rock. Then, before she could realize what was going to happen, Anne had turned and was hurrying towards her, her head down. There was no time to get out of her way. They bumped into each other. Anne slipped and fell into the icy rapids.

"Oh," she shrieked, "Oh, you!"

Jem pushed Phoebe aside, reached down, yanked Anne from the water, and turned to Phoebe. "What happened?"

"Spying!" Anne was gasping. "I told you! She was spying. She wants to kill me now!"

"Don't tell me now, you'll fetch pneumonia. Come on, run." Jem put his arm around Anne and, holding her close, rushed her towards the camp.

She hated Jem. Phoebe was full of such cold anger she didn't think she would ever care again what anyone thought of her. She hated Anne. She started up along the brook at a furious pace. Two small boys burst through the trees onto the patch in front of her. Johnny Anderson and Arnie Colliver.

"He does! He does so!" Arnie was shouting. "He likes me. He likes me better'n you. He lets me sleep all over his fur."

"He's jest nice, that's all. Phoebe told me he took a real likin' to me, and anyways you're a-scairt of him. I seen you jump back."

"I ain't a-scairt. You're a-scairt. Jest like your pa."

"My pa ain't a-scairt of nothin'. He's off fightin' with the Royals. You don't even know where your pa is!"

"I don't care! I don't care!"

The next words were lost as the shouting disintegrated into cries and grunts, flying fists, and kicking feet.

Phoebe dropped her bucket and pushed in between them. An arm grabbed her from behind and pulled her back.

"Let 'em be." Jem's voice was gruff. "They gotta fight out their feelings."

"They'll kill each other."

"Not them."

Phoebe did not want to let them be. She hated fighting; it frightened her. She did not want to stand beside Jem either, but since he wasn't moving and she couldn't leave the boys, she stood where she was, her back stiff, and said nothing.

The fight went on. The boys rolled over and over on the ground. They pounded. They kicked. They grunted. They cried. Blood spurted from both their noses. There was a scream of pain. Jem pushed Phoebe aside and lunged forward. He pried the boys apart. He hauled Johnny up by what was left of his jacket collar. Arnie tried to get up and fainted.

Phoebe ran to kneel beside him. "Jem, there's something wrong," she whispered.

Before Jem could say anything, Johnny threw himself down beside Arnie. "I killed him," he sobbed. "I killed Arnie."

"He ain't dead," said Jem, "he's just fainted. He's likely broke somethin'."

With a groan Arnie came to. He tried to sit up, but Phoebe put her hand on his chest and held him still. He looked up at her so trustingly that the anger that had consumed her such a short time before was dissolved.

Jem was right. Arnie had broken his arm. Lucy Heaton, who said she had set dogs' bones and, once, a horse's leg, set the bone, splinted it with two sticks, and wrapped it with a length of Arnie's mother's petticoat. Whisky from the flask she shamed her husband, Joseph, into contributing helped as anaesthetic.

And so the number of children by Phoebe's fire increased by one. Johnny Anderson, who now loved his friend Arnie as passionately as he had hated him earlier in the day, had to be carried kicking and screaming from Arnie's side by his determined mother. He was soon back. Although he slept by his mother and ate the corn porridge she made for him, he spent his days with Arnie. Mindful of his stricken face when he'd realized that Arnie had broken his arm, Phoebe could not send him away. Bertha Anderson decided Johnny was unlikely to get measles now. And so he stayed.

When Jem came by the next morning on his way to check his snares, Phoebe was sitting with Tibby's head in her lap, Betsy Parker clinging to one arm, and she was trying, with the other, to adjust the cloth that was wound around Arnie's splint. Jem grinned. "There was an old woman who lived in a shoe," he recited, "only you ain't so very old 'n' you ain't got a shoe to live in. But you sure got *so* many children. Here, Arnie, let me see that. I know how to wind them things." Jem knelt beside the boy and began, with deft fingers, to rewind the cloth.

Phoebe watched him covertly. Was she to take his banter for friendship? If he wanted to be friends with Anne and was willing to listen to those lies, she didn't know that she wanted his friendship. She felt so uncomfortable in his presence that she could hardly speak to him. As for Anne, she didn't want anything more to do with her. The rage she had felt at hearing Anne say those terrible things to Jem had gone, but she could not bear to look at her now. She remembered a line in a story her father had once told her about a bitter, stubborn old man who became a hermit. "The iron had entered his soul" was how the line went. Well, the iron has entered my soul, thought Phoebe, and I don't care.

The measles epidemic was passing. Even Tibby Thayer seemed to be over the worst, and everyone agreed that it was urgent they move on. Snow hadn't melted from the ground in weeks, and the ice was thickening on Axle-Broke Brook. They had been camped there for two weeks. It felt like two years to Phoebe. As Jem said, she was like the old woman in the shoe and she was tired of it — and sometimes resentful. She would awaken in the night, reach automatically for a stick to put on the fire, and think about Gideon's message in its pouch in the pocket tucked into her sleeve. I'll never deliver it to that British general, she thought despairingly. And she had no time for Bartlett or George, not that they had needed her attention. George left Jonah only to go hunting, and Bartlett — she hadn't realized it until Arnie insisted — Bartlett had disappeared.

They were eating their supper of beans and bannocks, huddled in their shelter, wrapped in blankets against the cold, the night before they were to break camp.

"We can't go without Bartlett." Arnie's eyes were full of tears.

"He ain't been here fer two days," said Jonah.

Phoebe didn't know what to do. She couldn't leave Bartlett out in the woods alone. Jem's eyebrow went up and he laughed when she said that. "Phoebe, you know bears sleep the winter through 'n' there's been snow flyin' for quite a time. I expect he stayed here a lot longer'n he should have on accounta he didn't want to leave you, 'n' mebbe the little 'uns, too, but I expect now he's gone off 'n' found himself a cave to sleep in."

"I don't know," said Phoebe slowly, "I guess I didn't want to think about him wanting to hibernate." Then she realized something else. "But, Jem, he will stay there all winter and, by spring, I'll be far away in Canada. He'll never be able to find me."

"Did you expect to keep him all his life, like a cat?"

"I never thought about it. But will he be all right without me? When he wakes up, will he be lonesome?"

"He's a bear, Phoebe, 'n' he's gonna be all growed by spring. Growed bears get along fine in the woods by their selves."

"But, Jem, I'm the only family he knows. He was still with his mother when she was killed."

"But, Phoebe. You're a good mama 'n' there oughtn't t' be a soul in all this rackety company who ain't grateful for it, but you ain't a mama bear 'n', what's more" — he grinned — "when Bartlett comes outta his cave next spring, it ain't his mama he's gonna be lookin' fer."

Phoebe knew what Jem said was true. Bartlett would be looking for a mate in the spring. But Bartlett. Bartlett was...Bartlett. Could he just go away like that and leave her? Her father, Gideon, Anne. Now Bartlett was gone.

"I know," Jem said ruefully, "he's been a better friend to you than anyone else. Well, mebbe the rest of us gotta be better friends to make up for him bein' gone."

"Phoebe, Phoebe, do you mean Bartlett's not coming back?"

"No, Jeddy." She tried to smile at her small anxious cousin.

"But."

"No, Arnie."

"Bartlett's gone to bed for the winter. Hold your jaws, all of you!" Jem said impatiently.

The children quieted, but they chose not to believe him. They took turns until late in the night calling him, watching for him. When morning came and Joseph Heaton, with much stamping and swearing, had managed to get his cart across Axle-Broke Brook, and the rest of the company started to follow him, the children set up such a howl for Bartlett that everyone stopped.

Old Aaron Yardley promised them a bear story — about hibernating. They didn't care. They would not be consoled. It was Joseph Heaton who got them going by bellowing at the top of his twangy voice that "every last bear in the dad-blasted Republic of Vermont will be on our tails on accounta they can't get no sleep with this caterwaulin' goin' on!"

The silence was so sudden and so complete that a single blue jay's call had the entire company looking up nervously.

The day did not improve. The children were too despondent even to fight. They sat in the carts, and almost the only sound heard from any of them all day was Tibby's cough. She had not recovered well from the measles, she had, in fact, developed a deep, wheezing cough that seemed to get worse and worse over the next two days as the refugees moved steadily north through the woods and over the frozen brooks. It snowed and sleeted, and the wind blew colder, and, all the time, Tibby became more listless. And, every time the Robinsons' cart went over a big tree root or the ox jerked, she shook with a paroxysm of coughing.

"That child is too ill to travel farther today," Rachael told Phoebe. The others agreed and, although it was only just past noon, they struck camp. There was no clearing, they were stopped on the path by a stream in a hollow so thick with huge pines that they had to worry about fires — nor were dry sticks easy to find. They crowded close together over three small fires. Over Joseph Heaton's grumbling, his wife, Lucy, gave Phoebe one of their quilts for Tibby. Bertha Anderson brought her a small jar of raspberry cordial.

"Here," she said, her voice gruff. "I was savin' this to celebrate with when we gets to Canaday, but the poor little soul might better have it." She thrust it into Phoebe's hand. She bent down and put her hand on Tibby's hot face. Tibby made no sign that she knew Bertha Anderson was there.

Phoebe tried to give her some of the cordial, but it was no use. She did manage to get two spoonfuls of hot water into her, but Tibby vomited them right back.

The other children gathered around silently, afraid to come too close, afraid to move away.

"Phoebe! Phoebe! Is she going to die?" Jed whispered in Phoebe's ear.

"No." Phoebe told him, her heart tight inside her chest. "No, she is not going to die. Of course, she is not going to die."

That evening the refugees shared their corn-meal samp, flavoured with a few beans from the dwindling supply. High in the pine trees the wind raged and the sleet pounded, but the evergreens were so thick they were warmer and drier than they had been for weeks. They spoke to each other that night with kindness. Even Anne and Charity Yardley did not whisper together like conspirators. They all knew that a greater enemy than wild animals or marauding soldiers stalked the land.

When it came time to settle, George, who had steadily avoided Tibby's embraces from their first meeting, curled up beside her. Jonah lay on her other side. Phoebe sat with Tibby's head in her lap all night. It was not enough. Through the night and the howling wind, Tibby grew sicker and sicker. Just before morning, without a whimper, she died.

The day dawned bright and still, but there was little brightness among the saddened refugees. Phoebe was stunned. She had really thought Tibby would get better. It wasn't that she had been unaware of the danger, but some of the other children had seemed as sick as Tibby and they had all recovered. There was something else. Tibby, so noisy and so stubbornly demanding, had found her way into Phoebe's heart without Phoebe realizing it. She realized it now.

As for the others, they mourned Tibby each in his or her own way. Jonah went limping off alone. Jed and Noah wouldn't leave their mother's side. Johnny Anderson, the Colliver children, and Jeannie Morrissay formed a tight knot, and Betsy Parker shadowed Phoebe's every move. Tibby's was the first death. The awareness of this was in everyone's eyes.

Bertha Anderson, in her blundering way, said to Phoebe, "I figgered if one of them orphans was to go, it would've been the other one. She ain't nearly so strong, though she's bigger'n what Tibby Thayer was." She swept her heavy sleeve across her eyes and sniffed loudly. Phoebe took Betsy's hand and held it tightly.

"Hush, now, Mistress Anderson didn't mean to be unkind," she said to Betsy later. "She's so busy grieving over Tibby she hasn't a moment to spare for you. You must not mind her. That tongue of hers runs around in her mouth like a cat chasing its tail."

Betsy gave Phoebe a tentative little smile.

Jem and Joseph Heaton dug a hole in the soft earth where an old tree had recently fallen. There they buried Tibby's body, wrapped in one of Bertha Anderson's petticoats. To everybody's astonishment, Phoebe's uncle roused himself from his torpor and, in a clear, deep voice, read the service for the burial of the dead from his prayer-book.

The rest of the day people spent drying out their sodden clothes as best they could by the three small fires, baking bannocks, and preparing to start out the next morning by first light.

Around sundown that evening, Phoebe sat alone by the grave, remembering Tibby saying to her, "You got me to look after," remembering, too, Bartlett clinging to her, letting her know, in his own way, that she had him to look after.

"And now you are both gone." She rubbed the tears from her eyes. She remembered something else: that last afternoon with Anne and Gideon. "War is so romantic," Anne had said. Phoebe's tears came, then, in a torrent she could not rub away.

She became aware, after a time, that someone was standing beside her. She looked up. It was Jem, carrying a small roughly carved cedar cross he had made to mark Tibby's grave. He sat down and put an arm around her.

"Oh, Jem, I don't think anything worse than this can happen. I really don't."

CHAPTER 12

The Prisoner

Early the next morning, when all the others were barely stirring, Phoebe went looking for something that might do for flowers to put on the grave. She broke the soft ends from a few cedar branches. Shivering in her blanket, she crouched down in the snow by a small rock pool in the stream. She was concentrating on finding a sharp stone to break the ice so she could wash, and didn't hear the whistling until it was quite near.

Someone was whistling "Yankee Doodle." Within seconds a young man appeared through the trees. He was dressed in a fringed deerskin hunting shirt and leggings, with high moccasins on his feet and a fur cap on his head, and he had a rifle over his shoulder. His whistling stopped abruptly when he saw Phoebe. They stared at each other.

Phoebe recovered first. She stood up slowly. Images raced through her head of the men she had run from with George and Bartlett, of the soldiers who had held the refugees at gunpoint while they stole their provisions. She would not let him see that she was afraid. She spoke without a quaver. "I am not alone. If I shout someone will come."

"I don't aim to do you no harm, Mistress. I'll just get myself gone before your friends get here." He gave her a little smile and turned to go. Too late. The sound of feet on the ice along the brook's bank was loud and clear. The young man started to run.

"Stop!" roared Joseph Heaton. He raised his gun. Jem sprinted through the trees, threw himself at the stranger, and brought him down by the knees. They tussled briefly, but Jem had the advantage of surprise and Joseph Heaton with his gun at the ready.

"You took me fair and square," the stranger conceded when Jem had taken his rifle and forced him to his feet. "But I got no quarrel with you, nor, I figger, do you got none with me." He looked over at Phoebe, a rueful expression in his dark eyes. "I wasn't about to offer no injury nor no insult to your sweetheart." Jem flushed. It took Phoebe a moment to realize what he'd said. Then all she could think was, What a notion! How that will anger Jem.

"Never mind that," barked Joseph Heaton. "You just best give out what you're a-doin' here, and right smart, too."

The young man said his name was Japhet Oram and that he'd been working for his uncle up on the Onion River but was on his way home to see his sick mother over the mountains in Bellows Falls, on the Connecticut.

Phoebe listened in silence as he told his tale. She knew he was lying. It wasn't just the momentary hesitation before he said Bellows Falls, it was the way he talked. There wasn't a settler in the whole Upper Connecticut River valley, her father had told her once, "who you can't identify by his speech." Japhet Oram did not speak with the clipped words or broad vowels she was used to hearing in Vermont. He had a slow, drawly accent, not one she had heard before. There was something else. Despite his hunting clothes and his ragged brown beard, he looked more like a soldier than a woodsman. It was the way he moved, and it was his black hair tied back in a neat queue. He looked like Gideon the day she had discovered him in her house in Hanover.

She said nothing about her suspicions. Japhet Oram didn't look to be any older than Jem — or Gideon. She didn't trust Joseph Heaton, and she wasn't sure Jem could stop him from shooting the boy where he stood if he thought he was a rebel spy. She thought, not for the first time, how Joseph Heaton reminded her of Elihu Pickens and the men on his Committee of Public Safety back in Orland Village. No, she would not say anything.

"We ain't settin' you free just on your say-so," snarled Joseph Heaton. He grabbed Japhet Oram's arms, pinned them behind his back, and held them there. "Who's to say you ain't a soldier of that dad-blasted rebel John Stark or Israel Putman? And who's to say you ain't a rebel spy? We ain't settin' you free."

"See here," Japhet Oram began, but Joseph Heaton paid no attention. He swivelled around to face Phoebe. "What's more," he snarled, "we ain't lettin' no one else set you free, neither." There was a look of such intense ill will on his face that, involuntarily, Phoebe backed away from him.

"You keep the gun on 'im," he barked at Jem and, pushing his captive before him, disappeared into the forest.

Phoebe felt sick. The look on Joseph Heaton's face had frightened her. "Jem?" she said uncertainly.

Jem had started after Master Heaton. He swung around. There was no warmth in his blue eyes now. "I don't think you're a spy, Phoebe Olcott. Not anymore. You know I don't. But I'd give a whole pound sterling if I had it to know what you 'n' that Japhet Oram was talkin' about."

"We weren't…"

There was no use explaining. Jem did not wait to hear. Phoebe pulled Katsi'tsiénhawe's blanket more tightly around herself, and stood, irresolute. She did not want to go back to camp. She did not want to think about Japhet Oram and what might happen to him. She looked down. She had not moved from the rock pool, and there, staring bleakly back at her, was her reflection in the clear black ice. "I do not want to think about you, either," she told it. She lifted her braid of matted brown hair and dropped it with a sigh. She looked at her tired, thin face, the hollows under eyes that were bigger and darker than she remembered. "I guess nobody could call me a plump partridge now," she said.

Back in camp Joseph Heaton had tied his prisoner's hands behind his back with a rope and was peppering him with questions. "Where were you? What're you *really* doin' out here? Why ain't a stout young feller like you in uniform? Where'd you get that rifle? It ain't commonplace around these parts." And on and on, until Charity Yardley said, acidly, "Master Heaton, if you are hoping for answers to your questions, you might give the young man time to respond."

With that, everyone had something to say,

something to ask. He told them his family were Loyalists. He told them again that he was going home to visit his mother. Nothing Japhet Oram could say would satisfy Joseph Heaton. "We knows you rebel spies. The general at Fort St. John's is goin' to be some happy to get a-hold of you," he crowed, "I wouldn't be a mite surprised if they wasn't willing to offer a nice reward." Almost everyone else wanted to let him go free. Bertha Anderson said she saw no reason why "half-starved folk like us should feed a healthy varmint like him," and, for once, Charity Yardley agreed with her.

Then Anne came forward to stand in front of their prisoner. "Don't you let him go." Her face was contorted with rage, her voice was shaking, her fists were clenched. "Don't you let him go. If he is a spy he must hang. Hanging is what happens to spies."

The look of sick terror that came over Japhet Oram's face was one Phoebe did not think she would ever forget, or the way his glance darted frantically from one person to another. In that moment she knew she would have to set him free. For a split second their eyes met. She did not dare look at him again.

Joseph Heaton's arguments won out. Japhet Oram was to be taken along to Fort St. John's. The snow and cold winter winds, Tibby's death, and now the capture of a man who might be a spy, gave the refugees a new sense of urgency. Quickly, they set to preparing the morning meal and assembling their possessions. While the cornmeal stir-about was being rationed out, Phoebe slipped away to the hillside where they had buried Tibby. She knelt by the cross Jem had made and laid there the bunch of cedar she'd been clutching since she'd gathered it by the pool. She prayed for Tibby's soul. Then she said, "Goodbye, Tibby Thayer. You were an odd, cross-grained little creature, and now the good Lord has taken you to be with your mama and your papa. I hope you are happier there than you were here." She wiped the tears from her eyes. She stood up — and saw Jem a few feet away.

Maybe it was the sadness of Tibby, maybe the capture of Japhet Oram, or the reliving of Gideon's hanging and Anne's hysteria, maybe the knowledge that Jem still distrusted her, but Phoebe was filled with a sudden, overpowering rage.

"What kind of spying do you think I'll be doing here?" She was so angry she spat out the words. She bent down, grabbed a loose clod of earth, and hurled it at Jem with all her strength. Then she burst into tears and ran, sliding and falling and bumping into trees, down the hill.

Much later, when she had calmed down and was pushing her way through the snow behind the Robinsons' cart, where Betsy rode with Jed and Noah, she remembered seeing pine cones and moss in Jem's hands. She felt ashamed that she had misunderstood, and she tried to tell him so, but whenever she moved up beside him to ask his forgiveness, he found a reason to busy himself somewhere else.

Bertha Anderson, with her ox and cart, now led the refugee party. Joseph Heaton brought up the rear with the prisoner, his hands bound in front of him, tied to the back of the Heatons' cart. The job of guarding the prisoner, Joseph Heaton told everyone, was not to be entrusted to a feeble old man like Aaron Yardley or a youth like Jem Morrissay. He only glanced disdainfully at Josiah Robinson and obviously did not consider that any of the women could do the job, so he had relinquished the lead position with reluctance, a shake of his fist, and the admonition to Bertha Anderson to "keep us outta the swamps and don't go gettin' us halfway up no mountains. And if you sees signs of catamounts 'n' such, you're to give a good warnin'."

Phoebe heard his loud complaints, his sharp orders to his wife and to his prisoner, but all she listened for was a silence that said he had left his post. He did that only twice in the day, but shouted for Jem to "come keep guard" while he disappeared to relieve himself. She knew she couldn't get near Japhet with Jem marching along beside him.

They plodded up steep hills in snow so thick everyone had to walk in order to lighten the weight in the carts. Now and then one of the mothers would insist that they stop for the children. Uncle Josiah leaned heavily on Rachael's arm. Jonah Yardley, on the other hand, seemed to gain strength from his very need of it, and he swung along on his crutches beside Phoebe with never a word of complaint, the cat by his feet.

Anne had withdrawn into herself once more. She no longer bothered with Jem. She no longer gossiped with Charity Yardley. Phoebe heard Charity say to Lucy Heaton that "the Robinson chit is the most unobliging human being I have ever met." She couldn't help smiling bitterly, but nothing could take her mind from Japhet for long.

All day and long after they had camped for the night, the question went round and round in Phoebe's head — how was she to free Japhet? Joseph Heaton never left the prisoner's side while they walked, and stationed himself near him once he had him safely secured to a tree after they'd stopped. If he left him for even a minute, Jem took his place.

Japhet. Phoebe had begun to think of him by his first name. It was as though, having made up her mind to rescue him even though he did not know it, there existed a bond between them. There was another bond. She didn't know where he had come from or anything about him except that he was not what he had said he was. She knew, though, that he was a prisoner and so was she. Unlike him, she was free to run off into the wilderness, but she was afraid of it. She no longer felt she would ever convince Anne that she was not the villain Anne thought she was. She had been thinking, for some time, though she still kept it in the pocket tucked into her sleeve, that she would never deliver Gideon's message in time to anyone who'd have any use for it. Tibby, who she had promised to care for, was dead, and although Betsy Parker had glued herself to Phoebe's side, she was sure that both she and Jonah would manage without her. No, she was not imprisoned by anything but her own terror of going out alone again into the wild. But the bonds of that prison were every bit as strong as the rope that tied Japhet. In a kind of way she felt that, if she freed Japhet, she was freeing herself — and Gideon.

When all the fires had burned low and people were restlessly settling down to sleep, Phoebe watched for her chance to creep over to where Japhet sat, tied to a large oak tree, hands and feet bound before him with the tough cedar-root rope the Mohawks called watapi. She could see, because the moon was full and it was a clear night, that he had fallen asleep. His head was hanging down, bobbing like an apple on its branch. Joseph Heaton was sitting a foot or two from him, his head nodding, too. Jem lay sleeping, the same distance on the other side. Phoebe thought desperately of creeping over to where they slept and knocking them both on the head with Charity Yardley's iron cooking pot. The only thing that stopped her was not knowing how she could hit one of them without the other one waking up.

I will have to be very quiet, she thought, and she was about to stand up when, as though reading her mind, Jem woke, sat up, and looked over towards where she sat. She could feel his eyes boring into her. She lay down, determined to keep awake, but, after a little while, she fell asleep — and dreamed that Joseph Heaton was riding on Bartlett's back, chasing Tibby and Gideon and Japhet with his hunting knife. Jem was running beside them, his coppery hair flying loose behind him.

She woke because Jem was squatting beside her, shaking her. "You was havin' a nightmare." She blinked and rubbed her eyes. There were tears. She sat up, shivering. She grabbed Jem's hand. "Why were you chasing them?"

"Huh?"

"You were, oh…" She shook her head. "It was the dream." She didn't move from his comforting presence until she realized she was holding his hand. "Thank you," she mumbled, pulling free.

"That's all right." Jem sounded as self-conscious as she felt. He got up and went back to his place by Japhet Oram. Phoebe pulled her blanket up around her shoulders, but she didn't sleep for a long time.

The second day was much the same as the first had been. Although the sun was bright, it was cold, and the going was all uphill in the snow. Jem and Joseph Heaton had a quarrel that stopped just short of a fist fight after Jem asked Japhet how near the Onion River they were, where it might be best to cross it, and what would be the best procedure north from there. Joseph Heaton told Jem not to "trust no dad-blasted spy." Jem muttered something Joseph said he hadn't any business saying in front of good Christian women. If Jem's mother and Bertha Anderson hadn't stepped between them, they might well have come to blows.

The first time Jem took his turn guarding "the spy," Phoebe could see by the expression on his face that he was more than a little tired of Joseph Heaton. She couldn't help but smile. Then suddenly Noah Robinson darted from his mother's side after a rabbit, fell in the snow, and started to roll downhill. Jem took after him. Phoebe slipped towards Japhet. She drew her knife from her sleeve just as Jed Robinson bounded towards her with the cat in his arms.

"Phoebe! Phoebe! I found George. He got

lost in the bushes." He pointed towards a clump of bushes leaning over the frozen stream that ran beside the hill they were climbing. Wondering where Jed found the energy, as thin and hungry as he was, Phoebe took the cat from him and made no further attempt to free Japhet.

Two near-fights among the boys were avoided by Bertha Anderson bullying Charity Yardley into taking some of the children into her cart once they reached the top of the hill. Johnny Anderson and Arnie Colliver were begging for something to eat, and Sam Colliver was whimpering that he was *so* cold. It was easy to see that trouble between some of the refugees could easily erupt.

As for Phoebe, all she hoped was that any one who had noticed her at Japhet's side would think she had simply wandered there.

But Jonah had noticed, after she had returned to his side and thrust George into his arms. "I see what you was gonna do," he told her in a low voice. A chill ran down Phoebe's spine.

"I won't tell," he said.

Phoebe looked at him, disbelieving.

"I can see this Japhet Oram isn't likely what he says he is. I'm hobbled in the leg, I'm not very old, but I'm not slow in my upper works." He grinned at her. "And I hate that old buzzard. He's not the king and he doesn't know all there is to know, and I don't want to see him win over anybody, not even General George Washington himself."

Phoebe squeezed his hand. She wondered if everybody else disliked Joseph Heaton as much as she and Jonah and, probably, Jem did. Jem. Phoebe was sure he had seen her slip in beside Japhet Oram, because every time she glanced in his direction he was looking at her with a thoughtful expression on his face. But he said nothing about it.

When, in mid afternoon the refugees reached a small beaver meadow, surrounded by a mostly evergreen woods, the level ground and the shelter the trees gave from the rising wind were too good to pass up, so they stopped there for the night. There was one large maple tree in the meadow at a little distance from the surrounding forest, and there Joseph Heaton tied Japhet.

Other than eating the small ration of beans Abigail Colliver fed him, and thanking her, Japhet said nothing and looked at no one, although Phoebe did think she saw him wink at Jed when Jed and Noah and Arnie Colliver stood in front of him and stared — before their mothers called them away.

Phoebe camped as near to the prisoner as she dared without attracting attention. Since she had Jonah and Betsy and the cat with her, she did not think anyone would notice.

Someone did. Anne. Phoebe was getting her fire going when Anne appeared beside her.

"I know what you mean to do, Mistress Olcott, and do not think for a single moment that you will get away with it. I mean to watch your every move. Every move! And you know what happens to traitors and spies," she hissed. With that she disappeared into the dark.

Phoebe went cold. Had Anne gone to tell Joseph Heaton what she suspected? Would he tie her up? Would be hang her on that tree? And Japhet Oram, too? Would all the others let him do that? She began to shake.

"Phoebe, I asked you three times, d'you want me to put these chokeberries in the beans?"

"I am the one slow in the upper works, Jonah. Yes, give Aunt Rachael whatever you've found for the pot." By this time three pots were all it took to cook what was left of the rations for everyone. So Phoebe had given up cooking unless the hunting and fishing proved successful.

Phoebe busied herself then, helping Aunt Rachael, settling the children, anything that would keep her mind off Anne — and Japhet. It was only when Betsy had been comforted one last time from the fear of the howls of wolves and the hooting of owls, and Jonah had pulled George close to himself in the cocoon he'd made of his quilt, that the full force of what she was about to do swept over her.

Free Japhet Oram? If she did not, he would surely be hanged. He would be hanged like Gideon, and it would be her fault if she could have freed him and didn't. No matter how she tried not to, her imagination would create his dead body swinging from the tree where he was now tied. But, every time she thought about freeing him, she shrank from it. She had come all the way over the mountains with only a bear and a cat to do one last service for Gideon because of the horrific thing that had happened to him. She had come along with Jem from Shaw's Landing on Lake Champlain because she had been afraid she would be hanged if she went home. How could she deliberately put herself into that danger now for someone she didn't even know? I can't do it, she decided. It probably is not true that he will be hanged when we get to Fort St. John's.

She lay down to sleep. But she couldn't sleep. The picture of Japhet's dead body swinging from the tree was too insistent. After at least an hour of this torment, she rolled over and looked across the few yards of meadow that separated her from the tree. The moon was hovering over the tops of the evergreens and she could see Japhet clearly. His head was nodding. Joseph Heaton was sleeping, soundly by the look of him, on one side of Japhet. Jem was sitting on the other side. He was sitting up straight, but every few minutes his head would nod. It was obvious he was having trouble staying awake.

Phoebe lay without moving, wishing the wolves would cease their dismal cries, her eyes shifting from Jem to Japhet to Joseph Heaton and back again, over and over. She knew that no matter how afraid she was, she was going to have to do this thing.

She waited. Half an hour went by. An hour. The moon was high in the sky and there was a cold stillness on the land. Jem's head nodded once, twice, and finally drooped on his neck.

Without really knowing what she meant to do, Phoebe reached out and grabbed a stick from the pile beside the fire. With the stick in one hand, her little knife in the other, she crept past Aunt Rachael and Uncle Josiah, past Mistress Yardley and old Aaron Yardley, to the edge of the meadow and around to the tree where Japhet was tied. Just as she reached it, Jem moved again. She didn't stop to think. She struck him on his head with her stick. He slumped over without a sound.

Swiftly and silently she moved to Japhet's side and began to slice at the *watapi* that bound his hands. He stiffened, struggled for a moment, realized what she was doing, and held his hands as far from the tree trunk as he could. It took an agonizing amount of time, but at last his hands were free. He grabbed the knife from Phoebe.

Within seconds he had the *watapi* cut from his ankles, and Phoebe had the rope untied from around his waist. He staggered to his feet, dropped the knife, and stumbled off.

For a moment Phoebe was too stunned to move, too stunned to realize that she had actually freed him. Then, like a fox on the run, she took off in the direction Japhet had taken. But as she reached the shelter of the trees, she stopped.

"Jem! Oh, dear Father in heaven, Jem!" she breathed. She dashed back to where he lay on the ground. She bent over him. She set her ear to his mouth, terrified she would feel no breath. He groaned and rolled, pulling her with him. She leapt up, her hand at her throat. He made no move. She stared down at him for one second. Then she turned on her heel and ran.

CHAPTER 13

One Is One

Phoebe sat with her back against an outcrop of rock. She drew her knees up to her chin and put her head down. Her muscles ached, her feet were sore, but with every ragged breath she breathed in the scent of pine. She closed her eyes and listened to the sounds of the waterfall far below. Above its roar she could hear the jays and crows calling to each other through the pines and spruces that grew down the sides of the gorge.

She had run from camp with no thought but to get away. She had paid no attention to where she was headed. She had broken through ice as she raced through streams, badly scratched her hands and face when she pushed hrough bushes, and torn her leggings scrambling up a bare hillside. She stopped on a small plateau beside which the river had cut a deep gorge in the mountain, and collapsed onto the ground against the rock. There was only one thought in her head, "I did it. I really did it." She said the words out loud and the enormity of what she had done began to sink in. She, Gideon's little brown mouse, had stolen up to Japhet Oram, tied to his tree, and cut his bonds. Whatever happened to him from now on, he was not going to be hanged.

"Phoebe! Phoebe Olcott! Don't you move. Don't you move!"

Phoebe leapt to her feet. She looked down the hill. The dawn light was pink but still dim. She could just make out the figure charging up the hill towards her, but there was no mistaking Jem's angry bellow.

"Don't you come a step closer, James Morrissay," she cried. "The other side of this hill goes straight down into a deep gorge. If you come one step closer, I'll jump into it."

Jem kept coming.

"I mean it." Phoebe took a step towards the cliff edge.

Jem stopped. He was three-quarters of the way up the mountainside now. "You won't get away." He shook both his fists at her. "I ain't gonna let you. You let that no-account rebel spy loose, 'n' you're gonna hafta answer for it! Your cousin Anne was dead-right all along. You had us all bamboozled with your bein' so nice to the children. And I thought, God Almighty, I was...

Oh, I could kill you." He started towards her again.

"I mean it. I'll jump. You won't have to kill me, you can just get yourself around by the bottom of the waterfall and gather up the pieces of me. I am not letting you take me back so you and Anne and your friend Joseph Heaton can hang me on that tree where you had Japhet Oram tied up. I'd sooner die here. Right now."

Jem stopped again. Phoebe could still see only the dark shape of him, his white face topped by his fur cap.

"I guess that's what you want," said Phoebe bitterly when he made no response. "You want to see me hanging from that tree. You want to watch my face go black and my eyes bulge out. Then you won't mind about Japhet Oram. Then maybe you won't mind about being put off your farm."

"Phoebe, no! I ——"

"Not one step closer. I'll jump. Then you won't have me to drag back to show what a fine hero you are. How did you find me, anyway, Jem?"

"You didn't hit me all that hard," he said impatiently. "I followed you. Phoebe, I ——"

"No, don't you speak." Phoebe took a deep breath. Leaning against the rock, exulting in her success only moments before Jem had appeared, something had happened to her. Something had settled inside her, a kind of understanding. And she felt now that, if she was going to die, she wanted Jem to know about it.

"All my life," she said, "I have never done a thing because it was only I who wanted it. My poor papa, who was so learned in Latin and Greek, would have gone hungry all the days of his life if I hadn't shoved a dinner dish under his nose every evening. I did Gideon's bidding because I loved him. I did Anne's bidding because I thought she was everything I should be. I so wanted to be like her! Gideon said I was his good-natured little mouse, but it was because I was willing to see the sun rise up from the river if he said it did. Anne thought the sun rose especially to light her path and I wasn't to block out its light. I was daft enough to think it was so. Daft, that's the word for me. There are others — cowardly, stupid. But you know, Jem, I do think Gideon was right, I think perhaps I'm good-natured, too. I let your family and Aunt Rachael convince me to come along with you not only because I was afraid to be alone in the forest — and the dear Lord in heaven knows how afraid I am — but because Aunt Rachael needed me and I felt so sorry for those children no one else cared tuppence for. I know how they felt and, if she had lived and I had lived, that little scrap of a Tibby Thayer would have had a place with me wherever I was to go."

Phoebe paused. She looked down at Jem. The sun was coming up behind his head, so she still couldn't see his face. All she could see was the outline of him with the fur of his cap like a golden fringe around his head. Behind him, in the distance, the hills and mountains ascended in layers, the rising sun resting on them like a flaming ball. The sky all around was the colour of deep-rose petals. It was so beautiful it hurt her to look at it on this morning.

"But now" — she swallowed — "but now I am going off to find Tibby where she has gone and I am going there without anybody's by-your-leave. It is a black and terrible deed to hang a person, Jem, and I figure the people who do that have God to answer to when they reach the next life. I could not be one of those people, Jem, nor have aught to do with them, so I cut Japhet Oram loose and I ran away. And if I have to die by my own choosing, though it be a mortal sin, I will do it, today, right now. I am fifteen years old. I turned fifteen the day we buried Tibby, though I did not think on it until this moment. Old enough. So if you've a mind to fetch me back to see me hanged, you can watch me pitch myself into that waterfall. You might like it every bit as much. You might."

"No," Jem shouted hoarsely. "No! Phoebe don't jump. I don't want… Phoebe, I promise, no one's gonna… I… oh, God, don't jump!"

"Jem, I am not coming with you." For a moment neither of them spoke. An early-morning wind soughing through the pine trees added a mournful note to the steady music of the waterfall. There was no other sound.

Finally Jem spoke. "Phoebe" — the crack in his deep voice was very pronounced. There wasn't a trace of anger in it — "Phoebe, I don't want… Phoebe, please don't jump. I won't ask you to come back with me if you think… Oh, damn, Phoebe." He pulled off his cap and ran his hand through his hair until it stood up like a hayrick. "Phoebe, I'll go back 'n' say I couldn't find you. But…"

"Why, Jem?"

"Why?" Jem's tone incredulous. "Why? Phoebe, I ain't never seen a body hanged 'n' I sure don't aim to start with you. I guess I don't care what you done, I ain't seein' you get hanged." His voice was shaky, and, in the growing light, Phoebe could see that he was clutching his cap to his chest as though he would save it, too, from that horrible fate. She took a deep breath. "So you mean to let me be?"

"What'll you do all by your lone self?"

"I'll do what I was doing before I found you by Lake Champlain. I'll make my own way."

"But you said yourself you was grief-crazed or you never coulda done it."

"But I did and I can do it again."

"It ain't safe, Phoebe, not for one girl alone."

"To my mind it's a lot safer than coming back to be with people with the intent of doing me harm."

"Not all of 'em."

"No, not all, but since everyone among you seems to do Master Heaton's bidding, I will not feel very safe. No, I don't belong with you refugees, Jem, because I was never forced out of my home. My father fought and died on the side of the people who did that to you. People you hate. My cousin Gideon was killed because he was a soldier for your side of the war. I picked up his spy papers, but I didn't pick them up because I wanted your side to win, it was because I needed to do it for Gideon. I set Japhet Oram free so he wouldn't be hanged, not because I'm for his side of the war — and I don't even know for certain which side he's for, nor do you. And, do you know, Jem, I don't care. I saw neighbours doing terrible things to neighbours back in Orland Village, and those neighbours who did those things do not seem to me to be any different from Joseph Heaton or Charity Yardley. Jem, I do not care who wins this dreadful war. And whoever wins it, I do not belong with you. I do not belong with the rebels. I do not belong with anyone, I think. But you do. Go back now, Jem, where you belong."

Jem didn't move. He stood there, clutching

his cap, staring up at Phoebe. "I can't just leave you." He took a step towards her. "Phoebe, I can't. And you ain't even got Bartlett nor George."

"No, I haven't."

"Phoebe" — his voice dropped so low Phoebe could scarcely hear him — "would… mightn't it be best if I was to come along with you?"

"What? What did you say?"

"I said I'll come along with you."

For a moment she could think of nothing to say, she was so dumbfounded. How could he say that after she had freed Japhet? After he had been so angry? After…after everything? It didn't make sense. He couldn't do it. "No," she said. "You have your way to go and I have mine." She paused. "Jem, it was good of you to say that, but you must go back now and keep your own promises." She turned to look down on the waterfall. The sun had just touched the mist over the cascade and it glowed with a deep coral light. On the other side of the gorge a doe stood sniffing the air around her. There was joy in her that she did not have to end her life there. She turned back to Jem.

"Goodbye, Jem. God keep you." She started up the hillside along the cliff edge.

"Phoebe!" Jem's voice was full of pain. "Phoebe, don't go! Phoebe, you do belong with us. Phoebe, I care about you."

Phoebe stopped, turned back once more, and said, "I care about you, too, Jem." Then she set her feet again in the direction she had chosen. She climbed until she reached the next plateau. There she stopped and looked back down the hillside. Jem had gone.

CHAPTER 14

The British Fort

It was on a morning more than three weeks later that Phoebe dragged herself to the shore of a wide river and collapsed. She was starving, she had cut one leg badly when she had fallen down a mountain crevice, and she was so spent she could no longer think.

Through the haze of exhaustion, she heard a startled exclamation, then a man say, "Lookee 'ere, 'ere's another of them half-starved refugees. Give us an 'and, will ye?"

Phoebe heard no more, felt no more, until she opened her eyes, many days later, although she did not know that then, to find herself staring up into a pair of anxious grey eyes. The eyes blinked in surprise, crinkled at the corners in a smile, and retreated.

"Plum tuckered out is all that's wrong," said a woman's deep voice, "that and a shortage of vittles. Now she's awake, better fetch up a bowl of broth from over to the mess."

Another voice answered, "Yes, ma'am." Phoebe drifted back to sleep.

The next time she woke it was dark and she was alone. She wondered where she was but didn't have enough energy to think about it. She learned later she was in the isolation hut because it was feared when she was found that she might have measles or smallpox or scarlet fever. It seemed as though only a moment had passed when she woke again, but she knew that was not so because there was light coming through the oiled cloth over the small window in the wall opposite. She was lying on a narrow cot built into the wall of a one-room log house. Against the wall, across from the foot of the cot, a fire was flickering in a rough stone fireplace.

That's good, she thought. She closed her eyes, then opened them again because she heard the creak of leather hinges as the door was pushed open. A kind-faced woman came in carrying a tray.

"Oh happy morning," the woman cheered. She threw off her shawl and picked her way across the room to the bed. "You've waked. Now don't you go back to sleep, dearie, not before you've had a wee sup of this good chicken broth. There's so little meat on them bones of yours, a starving wolf would turn up his nose at you."

Obediently Phoebe opened her mouth to the round pewter spoon thrust towards it. She was too weak to drink more than three mouthfuls, but they tasted so good and the broth smelled so good she asked if she might save the rest by her for later — and promptly fell asleep.

The next time she woke, she was alone again. A dim light was coming in the window and filtering through the chinks in the logs all around the house — and so were wind and snow. The smouldering fire sputtered on the hearth but shed little light and less heat. Phoebe shivered under the heavy blanket that covered her. Cautiously she lifted herself on one elbow. Her head felt as though it weighed fifty pounds, and she was dizzy. Little by little she forced herself to sit up. Slowly she manoeuvred herself to the side of the bed and put her feet to the floor. She jerked them back. There was a cold muddy puddle on the floor beside the bed. What's more, her right leg was throbbing. She gazed at it, puzzled. A length of lint bandage had been neatly wrapped around it. She sank back onto the bed. She remembered, then, falling down a deep crevice and cutting her leg on a sharp rock. She remembered, in vague snatches like a bad dream, the journey from the time she had parted from Jem on the mountainside. The days and nights did not seem separate, only moments — struggling across an abandoned beaver house, the sound of a catamount screaming, wolves howling, scrambling up a hill in the dark, the terror of the gleaming eyes all around her, the gradual realization that the hills had given way to low land, then a river where she had lain down to sleep, no longer caring what happened.

And, I'm alive and I'm here, she thought. But I wonder where here is.

Looking around her in the dim light, she saw that there was no furniture other than the bed and a small chest beside it on two planks to keep it out of the mud. The chest served as a bedside table. On it was the bowl of soup she had drunk from when she'd last wakened. There was a film of ice over it. Beside it lay her knife and her moccasins and, carefully folded, her tunic, her leggings — and her pocket. She wondered where her red blanket was.

She turned her attention to herself. She had on a homespun cotton bed gown, much too big for her. I suppose it belongs to the woman with the friendly face, she thought, absently rubbing the rough cloth between her thumb and forefinger. "I wonder if I am a prisoner here." She said this aloud and the sound of her own voice startled her. She pulled the cover up to her chin.

She didn't have long to wait to find out. There hadn't been time to more than imagine herself being dragged before a military tribunal made up of faces like Moses Litchfield's, Hiram

Jesse's, and Joseph Heaton's before there was a knock on her door and a small, thin Native woman came into the room. She was dressed in deerskin leggings and tunic, and had a red blanket around her like the one Phoebe had worn for so many weeks. Her black hair was in two braids down her back.

"Good morning," she said in Mohawk, and Phoebe responded in the same. The woman smiled and said something else, which Phoebe didn't understand. Embarrassed not to be able to reply, Phoebe asked if the woman spoke English, and quickly explained that, not only was she not Mohawk, she only knew how to say "good morning," "good night," and three other words. She pointed weakly to herself. "Kahrhakon:ha — a Mohawk boy calls me that. My name is Phoebe, but Peter Sauk says I am more like a sparrow than a phoebe."

"The English call me Mary Maracle." The woman smiled at Phoebe. "Like you, I have lost my home in this war. My brothers, my father, and my husband are fighting with Thayendanagea for the British cause. You are in good hands. My sisters and I are here at the fort to help the refugees who come."

"Fort. I am at a fort? What fort is it?"

"It is Fort St. John's on the Richelieu River."

She was in Canada! Fort St. John's was where the refugees — and Jem, Aunt Rachael,

Uncle Josiah and Anne — had been headed. But her relief passed quickly. Could they have arrived already? — how long had she lain ill? If they were here, they would have told the commanding officer about Japhet Oram. Had she been rescued only to be hanged? Would the commanding officer have mercy if she gave him Gideon's message? She looked over to where the pocket lay on top of her clothes. She had come so far, gone through so much to deliver that message. What if Anne or Joseph Heaton had already spoken against her? What if, after all this, she could never get that message to a British commander?

"I must see the commanding officer." She sat up. Too fast. Dizzy, she sank back down again. She sat up more slowly. "I must get dressed at once — I must go see the commanding officer."

Mary Maracle looked doubtful. "I think you will need to eat and rest before you are strong enough to go anywhere to see anyone."

Phoebe did not want to rest, she wanted to go at once to see the commanding officer, but when she put her foot out of the bed again a fresh wave of dizziness swept over her and she realized that Mary Maracle was right. Tears of weakness filled her eyes.

"Please," she said then, putting out her hand to clutch at Mary Maracle's skirt as she turned to leave. "Do you know of a party of Loyalists from Vermont?"

"There have been several."

"Is there a Mistress Rachael Robinson, or… a James Morrissay?"

Mary Maracle shook her head. "I have not heard those names — nor have we seen any new refugees these past few days — until you." She smiled. "You wait." Mary Maracle smiled at her again and quietly left the room.

Phoebe waited for what seemed like hours but was probably only ten or fifteen minutes. Then it was not Mary Maracle who came into the room, it was the grey-eyed woman with the kind face, the one who had brought the soup. She introduced herself as Lizzie O'Neil, the wife of a British sergeant.

"See the commanding officer, is it?" She looked quizzically at Phoebe. "Are you wantin' to tell me you're a King's scout, then? Does the King have girls in his army now?" She laughed.

Phoebe didn't know what to say. She didn't know what she could tell this woman, no matter how kind she had been. "No, no, but there was…there was a scout. He died."

"Oh, that's it, is it? Well, there's plenty of dyin' goin' on in these parts, surely. I'll see what I can do, but I don't believe you'll get to see General Powell. He's powerful busy, what with exchangin' prisoners and dealin' with refugees."

Lizzie O'Neil came over to the bed, leaned down, pulled the blanket up to Phoebe's chin, stroked her cheek, then left the room. But Phoebe barely noticed her leaving. General Powell, Lizzie O'Neil had said. General Powell was the general Gideon's message was addressed to. Of course, he would see her. It was *his* message.

The door blew open on a gust of wind and Mary Maracle came back in, interrupting her thoughts with a bowl of corn-meal samp, a basin of water, and a thin slice of soap. Phoebe ate a few spoonfuls of samp, then put the spoon down with a sigh.

"You cannot eat much when you have been nearly starved." And Phoebe understood by those words and the look in Mary Maracle's eyes that she really had been nearly dead, and why she was so very weak. She let Mary bring the basin of water to her in bed, and she washed her hands, treasuring the sliver of soap.

It was another day before she was strong enough to get out of bed for more than long enough to use the chamber-pot Mary Maracle brought her, or to have Lizzie O'Neil change the bandage and put fresh salve on her wounded leg. A long, impatient day. By the second morning she managed to eat all the samp in the bowl and, later in the day, to drink a whole cup of broth. Shakily, she got up to sit by the fireside that day. Sitting as close as she could to the feeble flames on a bench Mary had brought her, she washed her face, her hands, her neck, and her ears. How she longed for a whole tub of hot water in front of a blazing hearth fire in a warm room. And for clean clothes. Hers were stained and torn, the fringe on both tunic and leggings almost all gone, and so thick with dirt and sweat they seemed no longer to be made of deerskin — and they were now almost as much too big for her as the bed gown was. She slipped her feet into the moccasins that had little left to them but tops and only enough of their soles to hold in the pieces of blanket she had fixed them with. She remembered, then, sitting on a fallen log, cutting a length of blanket off with her knife, folding it to make soles to cover the holes in her moccasins.

For all her weakness, Phoebe did not let a chance go by to beg Mary or Lizzie O'Neil to let her see General Powell, and at last, when Lizzie O'Neil came in that afternoon, she was accompanied by a younger woman, a slim, pretty woman, her fair hair covered by a clean white cap. She had a bonnet over the cap and a green wool cloak over her shoulders. She put off her cloak and bonnet, laid them on the bed, and approached Phoebe in that same, quiet, competent manner Aunt Rachael had. The memory brought a tightness to her throat.

"This is Mistress Sarah Sherwood, Phoebe. Her husband, Captain Justus Sherwood, advises the General about all his scouts. His missus will see to it he gets your message."

"Oh, no!" Phoebe began — then, at the woman's shocked expression, remembered her manners and curtsied to her, although she felt foolish doing that in her leggings, and such manners seemed now to belong to a time long ago. "I don't mean to be impertinent, but mightn't I see General Powell, ma'am," she pleaded, "for I have a most particular message to give to *him*."

"I'm sorry, the General sees very few of us civilians. Your errand will be safe with my husband."

"But I must see him!"

"My dear child." Mistress Sherwood tucked a strand of hair into her cap impatiently. "I'm afraid General Powell really will not see you. I have come to you because I understand that you have been entreating daily, nay, hourly, to see him. It cannot be. The best you can do is to entrust your errand to a man he *will* see. That man is my husband. Captain Sherwood is a Loyalist soldier whose duty is to sort out refugees and scouts."

Still Phoebe hesitated. Could this Captain Sherwood see that Gideon's message would finally reach General Powell? Could he keep her from the wrath of Joseph Heaton and the others? Convince General Powell she was not a spy?

"Come, child," said Mistress Sherwood, "I cannot tarry here. I have left an infant waiting to be tended."

Phoebe looked from Mistress Sherwood to Lizzy O'Neil. There was nothing in the way either of them looked back at her to suggest that they might relent.

Phoebe made up her mind. "Then, please, let me come with you," she said.

Mistress Sherwood frowned, then nodded. "Here, now," Lizzie O'Neil held out a wool shawl. Phoebe took it, wrapped it closely around her shoulders, and followed the two women through the low wooden doorway. She stopped, blinking in the bright sunlight of a winter's day.

"Best of luck, dearie," said Lizzie O'Neil. She squeezed her hand and hurried off.

"Come." Mistress Sherwood took Phoebe firmly by the arm and began to walk briskly across the compound towards the west.

Phoebe's hut was at the south end of a compound, separated from the rest of the fort's houses and barracks by about two hundred yards, and she was more than grateful for Mistress Sherwood's arm as they walked. There seemed to be a great number of people, dogs, horses, carts, and oxen, and they seemed like a teeming multitude to Phoebe after her weeks alone in the wilderness. She looked around her, longing to catch a glimpse of her aunt or the little boys, but nervously half expecting Joseph Heaton to loom up before her, pointing accusingly. But there was no sign of any familiar face.

The fort stood on the edge of a broad river with only a road between it and the water. Across the river was a low ridge of land, above which Phoebe could see the roofs of houses. The land was cleared as far as she could see up and down the river. Inside the fort's enclosure were barracks where it appeared the soldiers lived, houses, warehouses, and a shipyard. At the north end was a big, square house which Phoebe took to be the general's headquarters. For one wild moment she thought of pulling loose from Mistress Sherwood's hold and dashing across the compound. But the impulse lasted only as long as the thought flitted through her head — she knew she couldn't run that fast, not in her weakened state.

Sarah Sherwood led Phoebe through the gate and into a village beyond, stopping only to identify herself to the soldier on duty. It seemed a place of great bustle and noise to Phoebe. She guessed there were about thirty or forty houses of stone or clapboard, a shop, and a church. The houses had high thatched or shingled roofs that curled up at their edges. Smoke rose from all their chimneys. The village looked prosperous and cheerful. It was not much bigger than the wilderness settlements Phoebe knew so well, but she thought it had a long-settled look.

"The village of St. John's was French until we won the war against them almost twenty years ago," said Mistress Sherwood. "Now there are as many English-speaking families as French here. Our house is there, see, just past the church."

The church was only a few yards farther down the road. Phoebe was in a fever to reach it, to make Captain Sherwood understand that she had to see General Powell, but she was so tired her steps were slowing, and she was afraid she would have to stop.

Mistress Sherwood paused. "Yes. You should not even be up from your bed, I am sure. And would not be if you were not so very determined." Her tone was disapproving.

Phoebe stiffened and forced herself to walk faster. In another minute or two they reached the dooryard of a small stone house where a tall, thin man dressed in breeches and shirt, was bent over a saw-horse, sawing the end from a wide plank.

"Justus," said Mistress Sherwood, "here is Phoebe Olcott, the young woman who was found half dead across the river, the same who has been plaguing our Mary Maracle and Lizzie O'Neil to see General Powell from the moment she opened her eyes on the world again. She would not entrust her message even to me to convey to you, but I think I have persuaded her that you are, indeed, the proper conduit. I understand from Lizzie O'Neil that she says a scout whose message it was is dead, but, here, she should tell her tale herself. Phoebe, my husband, Captain Justus Sherwood of the Queen's Loyal Rangers."

Phoebe gazed up into the Captain's politely questioning face. Her mind seemed suddenly to have stopped working. The moment had come after all this time, after all that had happened, the moment for her to give Gideon's message into the proper hands. And all she could do was stare. And think, irrelevantly, that his eyes were as blue as Jem's. "Captain Sherwood," she said, at last, in a small voice.

"As you see." He smiled. He turned to his wife. "Sarah, I think the child needs to sit down and could perhaps do with a sup of tea and a bite to eat. Come, Mistress Olcott. Yes, my wife is right. Any message to General Powell comes to me first. After a bit of sustenance, you will tell me your story. It can wait that long, I feel sure." Justus Sherwood spoke like a man used to having his wishes obeyed.

Phoebe realized then that she did feel faint and that she was hungry, but she couldn't eat, she couldn't wait a single moment longer. She sat down on the edge of the settle that stood at right angles to the fireplace in the front room of the little house. Captain Sherwood sat himself in the ladder-back chair across from her.

Phoebe leaned forward on the settle and

took the by-now threadbare pocket from her sleeve. With a hand that shook, she unfolded the sheet of onion-skin paper that she had found in the hollow tree and gave it to him. She told him her story from the time she had found it — though she did not tell him about Gideon's visit to Polly Grantham. As briefly as possible she recounted her journey over the mountains, about meeting Jem and discovering that Fort Ticonderoga was deserted, about travelling with the Loyalist refugees. Then, looking steadfastly down on her tightly clasped hands, she told him about the capture of Japhet Oram, about setting him free and then running away. When she had finished, she leaned back again and closed her eyes. She felt, rather than saw, Sarah Sherwood come and sit beside her.

"You have had an ordeal," she said softly, "but you are among friends here."

"Oh, but" — Phoebe swallowed hard — "there is something else. My father was a rebel. He...he was killed in battle in Boston two years ago. I do not turn away from his memory. I know he believed he did what was right — and I love him for that. I do not feel dishonoured by his embracing that cause. It was not mine, no cause is mine, I think, but I...I think you will not wish to number one such as I among your friends."

Sarah put an arm around her. "Justus was

once one of Ethan Allen's Green Mountain Boys — the same Green Mountain Boys who have now taken so much from us Loyalists in the name of liberty for their Vermont Republic. He changed his thinking. But Justus's uncles are passionate rebels, while Ethan Allen's own brother has been known to work for the British. The Wallbridge family, all but Elijah, are rebels — yet Elijah is with us. It is so in all the King's American colonies. We are as divided as a family of quarrelsome goats.

"There was a time" — she sighed deeply — "when we thought the rebellion would not last longer than a few months. Then we would all go home and make peace with our old neighbours. Now we can see that the war will not be soon over and, should the rebels win, we may never go home. Providence alone knows what will become of us."

Captain Sherwood came and took Phoebe's hand. "I knew your Gideon Robinson," he told her. "I'm sorry."

"Oh, did you?" Phoebe looked up into his compassionate eyes. "Was he…was he…?" Her throat was so thick with tears she couldn't go on.

"He was a good soldier."

Neither of them said any more. But Phoebe couldn't help wondering if Justus Sherwood was thinking, too, that it wasn't good soldiering of

Gideon to be home in Orland Village when he should have been miles away, heading towards Lake Champlain.

"Now," Sarah Sherwood said, "it is time to remember you are not the wild forest creature you resemble. It is time for a bath, a proper meal, and time to lose these leggings and put on a gown again."

"First," Justus Sherwood said, "I believe this young woman will wish to know we've received a report that the friends with whom she travelled so long are safe — they have arrived in Fort Sorel on the St. Lawrence River."

Phoebe leapt to her feet, exhaustion forgotten for the moment. "Aunt Rachael? Is Jem — is my aunt there? Is Anne? — Are they...?"

"It appears that a certain Farmer Heaton," continued the Captain, "seems to believe you are a dangerous rebel spy. I took his story to General Powell, but neither the general nor I was convinced that a young girl freeing a handsome youth meant she was a spy."

"Well, I am not!"

"No," the Captain agreed. "Furthermore, not all in Farmer Heaton's party felt as he did. A young man named Morrissay seemed prepared to do battle with all comers in defence of you."

"Oh," said Phoebe, "does Jem really...?" Her heart felt suddenly too full of gladness to say any more.

"You are an astonishing young woman, Phoebe Olcott" — Captain Sherwood smiled at her — "Were you a soldier under my command, I would be much inclined to recommend you for a promotion for bravery in carrying out the mission of a dead comrade. But, as I cannot do that, I will see to it that you are well fed, and clothed as well as this impoverished establishment can afford, and send you north to Fort Sorel by the earliest conveyance moving in that direction. Fort Sorel is where refugee families must wait the war out and you will be with your family there.

"I will inform General Powell of your adventure and of your steadfast courage in seeing your cousin's mission accomplished. I will give him the message you carried so faithfully." He took Phoebe's hand again and shook it, put on his coat, and went out.

Phoebe sat down on the settle, suddenly aware of how very tired she was. She had finally reached the end of the journey that had started at the hollow tree. She had done for Gideon what she had set out to do. She knew now that she had done it for herself, too, and for her father and for all that he had cherished — loyalty, trust, the keeping of promises. How very much she had learned from her quiet scholarly father! She felt, too, that with the telling of Japhet Oram's escape, she had laid a fear to rest

— the Sherwoods had not turned against her. But even if they had done, she knew that if she could go back to that moment when she had cut his bonds from him she would do it again.

The next few hours were completely blissful. While Sarah Sherwood nursed her two-week-old infant in the front room, a servant girl brought a large tin tub into the kitchen and set it in front of the dancing flames in the big fireplace. She filled it with steaming water and set a screen around it. She gave Phoebe a cloth and a large slice of strong soap, and Phoebe scrubbed her body and her hair free of two months of dirt. Looking at the bath water afterwards, she decided that the Sherwoods, if they had a mind to, could grow cabbages in it, it was so thick and black. It was the first spark of humour she had felt since the night she had fled the camp.

Sarah Sherwood gave her one of her own shifts and an old wool gown. It had once been blue, she told Phoebe, but it had been washed so often it was now the soft blue-grey colour of a nuthatch's wing. It smelled of the wild thyme it had been laid away in.

At Sarah Sherwood's bidding, she sat down at the deal table in the middle of the warm kitchen and ate a meal of roasted pork and potatoes and sauerkraut. She thought she had never said a blessing before a meal with more gratitude in her heart.

CHAPTER 15

Will You Wait?

The journey from the rapids at Chambly to Fort Sorel on the St. Lawrence seemed like a holiday to Phoebe. She hadn't minded the twelve-mile trip from Fort St. John's to Chambly, riding pillion behind one of the soldiers on his horse, but the trip on the big, flat-bottomed bateau down the Richelieu River was a joy.

It was a clear December day. The sky was bright blue and cloudless. A few small birds fluttered in the bare branches of the towering hardwood trees along the shore. The wind was cold, but Phoebe was warm. Sarah Sherwood had given her an old but still serviceable hooded brown wool cloak to cover her tunic and leggings. She had given her the shift and the blue gown, too, but Phoebe had wanted to wear Katsi'tsiénhawe's clothes. She had washed them and spent painstaking hours mending them because they felt like a talisman, a safe conduct from Peter Sauk and his family. So, while she had accepted the gown gratefully, she had worn the deerskin clothes despite Sarah Sherwood's disapproval. Mary Maracle had made her a new pair of moccasins.

Now, wrapped warmly in the cloak, the hood pulled up around her face, Phoebe stood at the railing of the boat and gazed at the country around her with keen pleasure, lazily aware that she did not have to keep all her senses alert for signs of danger. She paid scant attention to the soldiers talking among themselves. The Richelieu, slow moving through this low land, was a beautiful river, although, she thought, not as beautiful as her own Connecticut, fast flowing through the high hills. It was frozen over now, except for a channel barely wide enough for the boat. The boat's captain said that a few more bitter-cold days would close the river for the winter.

He told her that people had been settled along this river for a long time and pointed out well-established French villages on either shore. Smoke rose from chimneys, and she could distinctly hear the creaking of mill wheels, the jingling of sleigh bells, the neighing of horses, the lowing of cattle, and the sound of human voices over the water. She wondered what it might be like to live in a place where generations of one's own people had lived, where the forest had been shoved back, leaving no trace of itself, where the land had been tilled for so long it only waited for the farmer every spring to make it ready for a new crop. She could see, in the frozen fields, the stubble of last summer's Indian corn.

She thought about the French people who lived on these farms, in these villages, who had lost their war and now had to be loyal to the English king across the ocean, a king who didn't even speak their language. Loyal. That word that caused so much trouble. Loyal. How could people feel loyal to a king they didn't know, who lived in a far-off country, even when he did speak their language? Wasn't it more important to be loyal to what was right or to those people you knew and cared about? What was the good of killing people or being hateful to them because someone you didn't know was doing something hateful to someone else you didn't know? She grieved for her father dying in Boston for his strong belief in an idea of freedom, and Gideon for a king over in England. She grieved for Deborah Williams driven from her home, for Aunt Rachael and Uncle Josiah, for Jem, whose own father had gone off to fight in the Royal Yorkers and might be alive or dead, and for Tibby Thayer.

"It's true what I said to Jem," she whispered fiercely to herself. "It really is true. I don't care,

I cannot care who wins this war." But she realized she did care about the war's refugees — those refugees she had travelled with for so many weeks. Had they all survived? Would they despise her? Would Jem — in spite of what Captain Sherwood had told her and what Jem himself had said on that hillside by the waterfall? Aunt Rachael, she felt sure, would never turn away from her, nor Uncle Josiah, though he was all but witless now. She did not think about Anne.

She brought her thoughts back to the river billowing up around the sides of the boat. It was mid afternoon. The boat was nearing Fort Sorel, where the Richelieu flowed into the St. Lawrence. That great river glittering under the sun, the ice, tossed up on shore by the wind and the moving water, looked from a distance the way Phoebe had always imagined castles to look.

"It must be as big as the ocean!" Phoebe stared at the expanse of it in amazement. She realized she had spoken aloud when a voice responded.

"Not here, Mistress." One of the soldiers had come to stand beside her. "Northeast of here she gets even wider, and on up by Quebec she gets salty and then she's more like the ocean. It's mighty fine up there, where the wind sings loud and high through the big pines and along the rocky shore."

There was a wistful note in his voice that caused Phoebe to turn and look at him more closely. He was thin and young with straw-white hair. He was dressed like so many of the Loyalist soldiers she had seen at Fort St. John's, in a patched dark blue uniform coat and shabby linen leggings that had likely been buff-coloured but were a sort of nondescript tan now.

"Do you come from near the ocean?" she asked.

"Yup. I come from Maine 'n' I'd give three years of my life and a good bull calf to be back there now."

"Why aren't you?"

The soldier sighed. His shoulders slumped.

"I'm sorry." Impulsively Phoebe put her hand on his arm. "But I don't understand what snags so many men and boys into going to war. I really don't."

The soldier sighed again. "I reckon fer me 'twas when the mob stripped the clothes off old Obadiah Hanks and slathered him with hot pine pitch and rolled him in chicken feathers, then rode him around on a fence rail 'til he screamed. He hadn't done nothin' but call them a clutch of rowdies and roughnecks. That set my blood a-boilin' and I lit into Billy Pierce, and it wan't but a sneeze-up afore the whole clanjamfry of 'em was after me. I lit outta there lickety-split. I was set to hide in the woods fer a time and then go on home, but I was so riled, I up and took myself up to the St. Lawrence River and marched all the way to the British holdings at Three Rivers here in Canada and," he finished on a low, sad note, "I joined up with 'em."

"And now you hate it."

"Wal, I don't see the use of it, much. I been in Gentleman Johnny's army alongside of Captain Sherwood and Colonel Peters and the rest in this here Queen's Loyal Rangers and I seen things worse than what happened to old Obadiah Hanks. What I ain't seen is, I ain't seen anything to make me doubt we'd all be a sight better off gettin' the hell outta here and goin' home, beggin' your pardon, Mistress.

"My ma used to break up fights between my brother Dan and me. She'd set us to polishin' the front window, one on one side, one on the other. We would of give up teeth to bust that window and have at each other, but the wrath of our ma wan't a thing to play light with. So we polished and we polished, and by 'n' by, we began to feel so foolish we'd have to laugh. Well, mebbe this here war needs my ma to set us all to polishin' windows."

Phoebe had a sudden picture of General Powell, Captain Sherwood, Joseph Heaton, and a thousand others lined up along one side of an enormous glass window with an equal number of angry rebel generals, soldiers, and Sons of Liberty on the other, all polishing away. She giggled.

The soldier grinned. "I guess it ain't such a practical notion. Anyways, here we are and I got chores to do before we tie up. I wish you Godspeed, Mistress."

"Goodbye. Thank you for keeping me company — and for making me laugh. I am Phoebe Olcott from over on the Connecticut River, in Vermont. If...if you tell me your name I will keep you in my prayers," she said shyly.

The soldier smiled at her and suddenly he looked very young. "Well, Mistress Phoebe Olcott, I'd take that most kindly. My name's Ben Larkin." He took her hand and shook it vigorously. "When I'm up here to Sorel again I'll come see how you're fairin'."

Ben Larkin's window polishing and his warm smile had made Phoebe a little less worried about facing Fort Sorel and her old travelling companions, and she looked with open curiosity towards the fort that would probably be her home for the duration of the war.

Fort Sorel stood on the western shore of the Richelieu, where it met the St. Lawrence River. Except that it was open to the water on two sides, it was much like Fort St. John's, only larger. There seemed to be more barns, more houses, more barracks, and the shipyard was bigger. But it was so like the place she had just left that Phoebe almost expected to see the faces she had been used to seeing during the two weeks she had been at Fort St. John's. And, in a way, she did. There were soldiers, dressed in all manner of uniforms, some wearing bandages, some using walking-sticks. And there were the refugees with the same bewildered look, like children set down in unfamiliar surroundings without their mothers. With her cloak drawn tightly around her, her bundle of clothes under her arm, Phoebe marched bravely down the gangplank towards the big building at the west end of the compound that looked to be the fort commander's headquarters. She had, carefully tucked inside her sleeve where she could feel the crackle of it, the letter on heavy, official stationery that Justus Sherwood had put into her hands early that morning.

She was threading her way through the knots of people, the carts and horses, when she heard someone cry out her name. She whirled around. It was Jem. Tall, lanky, his light-red hair flying loose behind him, he was racing towards her. In one swift move, he threw his arms around her, lifted her off her feet, and hugged her so tightly she could hardly breathe. He kissed her all over her face, her eyes, her nose, hugged her again, then set her back on the ground but did not let her go.

"Phoebe, oh Phoebe." He was trembling

and his voice was husky. "I thought…I thought …Oh, Phoebe!" His face was wet with tears. He hugged her again, until she had to cry out. He loosened his hold. "Oh, God, Phoebe, I thought you were dead."

"I…I'm not." Phoebe hugged him tightly but quickly around his waist. She was happy, she was embarrassed, and suddenly she didn't know what to do. No boy had ever kissed her, no one had ever shown her this kind of affection. She was quite overcome. Jem stepped back and hastily drew his sleeve across his eyes.

"I'm all right, Jem," she said breathlessly, trying to cover her confusion. "I wasn't, because I hurt myself and I nearly starved, but then I got to Fort St. John's — no, that's not so, I almost got to Fort St. John's, when some soldiers found me, and then there was Mary Maracle and Lizzie O'Neil who took care of me, and Mistress Sherwood and Captain Sherwood — and she gave me a gown but I didn't want to wear it because Peter's sister gave me these clothes but I have it anyway and I was so worried about coming here but a nice soldier named Ben Larkin made me laugh about polishing windows ——"

"Whoa!" Jem grinned at her. He put out his arms to pull her to him. He dropped them to his sides. He flushed and stuffed his hands in his coat pockets. "What are you talking about, Phoebe?"

"I don't know." She started to laugh. Jem started to laugh. They looked at each other, then looked away. They laughed again for the sheer joy of finding each other. Finally their laughter subsided, leaving them both a little less self-conscious. Phoebe became aware again of voices, of people coming and going, of a horse whinnying.

"Jem" — she paused hesitantly, afraid of what she might hear — "is everyone all right? Did everyone reach here safely?"

The lingering smile left Jem's face. "Not everyone." He sighed. "Phoebe, your uncle Josiah got all the way here, but he died only a few days after. He was just plum wore out, your aunt said. Anne took it hard."

Uncle Josiah. He had always been such a shadowy figure in the family, quiet, studious, always a little frail. Phoebe felt the tears rising in her to think of him dying so far from home, so far from his books and the work he loved so much. She remembered Aunt Rachael saying once that Uncle Josiah ought never to have left Connecticut. Now he was gone.

Jem took her bundle from her and they walked together across the hard-packed snow towards a log barracks along the south wall of the enclosure. Jem said it was where the Vermont and New York refugees were housed.

"And there ain't but the one room fer us all," he grumbled. "But then there's folks come after us who's got to live in tents." He pointed towards the west end of the compound where half a dozen tents were set up. "They'll get buildings soon enough, but the General don't know what to do with us all," he went on. "There's so many of us and there's more comin' every day. And we sure don't know what to do with ourselves. Ma figgered things was gonna be dandy if we could just get ourselves into this British-held country. Well, here we are but I've heard tell that Governor Haldimand over in Montreal thinks for sure some of us is rebel spies, so he's plannin' to set up a Loyalist camp over in a place called Yamachiche on the other side of the St. Lawrence so's we'll all be farther away from rebel country, where we can't do no harm."

"Why would there be spies? What could there be to spy on here in a Canadian camp full of refugees?"

"Well it ain't just refugees here, there's soldiers. This here's a proper fort. Over in Yamachiche across the St. Lawrence, there'd be just you refugees."

Phoebe turned his words over in her mind. She stopped walking and turned to Jem. "'You refugees'?" she said. "What do you mean, 'you refugees'? You're one, too."

"Phoebe, there's a thing I got to tell you." Jem gripped her hand. He looked at her, then looked away. "I've joined up."

"Joined up?"

"Phoebe, I told you. I told you way back when we was gettin' ourselves from Lake Champlain to find my ma. I told you I was itchin' to join."

"Yes, but..."

"And I figgered my ma was safe here 'n' would do well enough without me. And I thought you wasn't ever comin' back." He took a deep breath. "And, anyways, I done it." He looked at her apprehensively. After a long wait he asked, "Ain't you gonna say somethin'?"

"No." What could she say? She couldn't even think.

He grimaced, looked at her as though he wanted to say something more, sighed, and started walking again.

Inside, the barracks was, as Jem had said, one large room, about twenty feet long and not much more than half of that wide. It's naught but a covered campground, thought Phoebe. But no campground had ever been so smoky or reeked so of unwashed clothes, unwashed people, stale food, and old smoke. The fireplaces at each end of the room sent out almost no heat and a lot of smoke to add to the stench. What fresh air there was seeped in through the chinks between the logs and around the edges of the door, and the windows, one on either side of the door.

Phoebe pulled her cloak up to cover her nose as she looked around her. Through the haze she could see all the people she had so dreaded meeting again. But now the dread was gone, altogether gone. She was glad, glad even to see Joseph Heaton's sour face turned towards her in shock.

Before Master Heaton had time to say a word, Betsy Parker caught sight of her. She hurled herself at Phoebe. Phoebe swung her up into her arms. Over Betsy's head she saw Jonah Yardley grinning at her. In his arms he held George. Phoebe's eyes filled.

"I'm happy to see you, Jonah." She smiled tremulously. "And George, too."

"Yes, ma'am." He put the cat down and came swinging towards her on his crutches. He held out his hand. Phoebe took it and squeezed it hard. "Come," she said. With Betsy Parker cradled in one arm, Jem on one side of her, Jonah on the other, she started towards the far corner, where Aunt Rachel had risen from a chair and was moving towards her.

"Just a minute, Mistress Phoebe Olcott." Joseph Heaton shoved Jonah aside so forcefully the boy almost fell. He grabbed Phoebe by the arm and spun her around. Betsy cried out.

"You got more gall than the whole dad-blasted rebel army, marchin' in here sweet as you please as if we didn't know what you done.

You're a traitor and a spy and we don't want you in here with us honest folk. We want you locked up and dealt with like the rest of the spies, and I'm a-gonna see to it that's where you gets to."

Jem grabbed Joseph Heaton by the shoulder. "Let loose her arm," he snapped.

Phoebe set Betsy on her feet, pried Master Heaton's hand loose, and held out her own hand.

"How do you do, Master Heaton."

"Don't you how-de-do me," he snarled.

By now the entire room was silent. People were moving towards their voices. Betsy clung to Phoebe's leg. Jonah took her hand. Jem put his arm around her. Phoebe's mind flashed back to the night she had arrived at the first camp, when Anne had screamed at her. She had been alone then. She was not alone now.

"Master Heaton," she said, "I am not a spy and I am not a traitor. I have a letter from General Powell at Fort St. John's to say that this is where I am to come and this is where I am to stay until the war is over. He knows all that I have done. He has no wish to see me imprisoned."

"The General don't know what us knows and, what's more, I don't see no letter."

Phoebe pulled the letter from inside her sleeve and held it out to him.

"I cain't read in this kinda light," he

growled, "Here, Lucy, your eyes is better nor mine, you read it."

Lucy Heaton came to stand by her husband. She smiled timidly at Phoebe. Phoebe smiled back and handed her the letter. Lucy read aloud the words Justus Sherwood had asked General Powell to write, words that commended Phoebe for her courage and perseverance in carrying the message entrusted to the scout Gideon Robinson. The letter ended by asking Fort Sorel's commander to give her "succour and asylum" for as long as she should have need of it. It was signed "Brigadier-General Watson Powell, Commander, Fort St. John's."

When Lucy finished reading, she handed the letter back to Phoebe. "Here, child," she said quietly, "you will need this to give to the commander."

Joseph Heaton seemed to shrink a little. He glared around the room, looking for support, but every single person there stared back at him coldly — even Charity Yardley. "Hmpf!" he said. "Letter or no letter, I has my suspicions."

"Well now." It was Bertha Anderson. "I knowed all along you was a good girl in spite of what some of them said. I knowed all the time else I could never have trusted you to care for Betsy here, or poor little Tibby Thayer who died. I, for one, am glad to see you come back to us safe and sound."

"And you must come now and see your aunt and sit a spell and tell us how you fared." It was Peggy Morrissay, taking advantage of the moment Bertha Anderson had stopped for a breath.

"Thank you." Phoebe smiled gratefully at Jem's mother. Still holding Jonah's hand, with Betsy still clutching her leg, Jem beside her with his hand under her other elbow, she made her way to where Aunt Rachael stood waiting. Anne stood at her side. The little boys, open-mouthed, stared up at her from the floor, where they were playing with a set of roughly carved wooden soldiers.

"I am sorry, Aunt Rachael." It was all she could think to say.

Aunt Rachael didn't say anything. She took Phoebe in her arms. When they drew apart, Aunt Rachael put her hand out and smoothed Phoebe's soft brown hair back from her face. "I see you still wear your Mohawk friend's dress," she said.

Phoebe smiled through her tears. She looked at the bundle Jem carried in his hand. "I have a gown," she said, and Aunt Rachael smiled back. "So," she said, "your mission is complete." And Phoebe knew that Aunt Rachael understood why she had freed Japhet Oram.

In a small, quiet voice Phoebe didn't think she had ever heard her cousin use, Anne asked, "Phoebe, what did the General mean about 'Gideon's message'?"

Phoebe looked at Anne. She looked at Aunt Rachael, at Jem, at the children, at the other people gathered around, people who had once felt she had betrayed them, people with whom she was going to have to live for months, maybe years more. So she sat down on a bench near one fireplace and she told them all about finding the message in the hollow tree. "And I hated them," she said. "I hated them who had hanged Gideon, and I wanted...I wanted..." All the feelings she had had on that bleak and terrible morning came back. The tears poured down her face and choked the words from her throat. She took a deep breath and went on. "I was afraid, but I had to do it for Gideon because I loved him. And because he was loyal. How could I be other than loyal to him in this one last thing. And because, Anne, because you said I was a rebel and it was my fault. So I took it. I took the message and I followed the brook, as Gideon once bade me."

No one listening made a move or a sound while Phoebe told about George, about Bartlett, about Peter Sauk and his mother and sister and all that happened before she met Jem and discovered that there was no one at Fort Ticonderoga to give Gideon's message to.

"And so I came along with Jem and you were all there, and now, I guess, I'd best find the fort commander and give him my letter and learn what he means me to do. I trust I am a refugee, now, too." Gently she removed Betsy's hand from her leg where it had been resting all through her story, and stood up to go. Jem was watching her intently, and she wanted to say something to him, something about why she had not felt able to tell him her story when they were coming through the forests together, but she couldn't seem to form the words.

She hadn't taken more than a few steps beyond the door when a barely audible voice behind her made her stop. She turned. It was Anne, and Jem was behind her. Anne wore no cloak against the cold, her face was pinched, and her violet eyes were dark with an expression Phoebe didn't understand.

"Why did you not tell me?" The question was not a reproach. Anne really seemed not to understand. Behind her Jem slipped off into the twilight. Neither girl noticed him leaving.

"I couldn't. You were so angry. You thought it was my fault. I couldn't talk to you. You wanted to see me hanged. I was afraid of you."

"Did...did Gideon's note say your name?"

"No. No, it didn't. It said for whoever found it to take it to Elias Brant or ——"

"But he was my brother. I should have...I would have taken it and I would have taken you with me!"

"Anne, I..." Phoebe was stunned. Not once

from the moment she had discovered the tiny silk-wrapped message and Gideon's note had she thought that she and Anne might have braved the mountains together. She had not thought, either, of what Anne might want or how she might feel. She had been so devastated by everything that had happened that she had thought only about her own feelings, her own fears. In fact, she realized suddenly, she had never considered Anne's thoughts or feelings about anything. She had always been in too much awe of her. But Gideon had been Anne's brother, and maybe if she had told Anne about the message, maybe everything would have turned out differently.

She felt her face grow hot. She didn't know what to say. She put out her hand, drew it back. "I...I'm so sorry," she mumbled. "I should have told you, but you were so...oh, I should have told you! I'm sorry."

Anne took Phoebe's hand. She was trembling. "I...well...I..." Her voice faded. She stared at Phoebe, her eyes full of tears. "I was mean and spiteful to say those dreadful things," she whispered, "and...and I...I think maybe I would not have been brave enough to have come with you. No, I don't think I could do what you did."

"I couldn't either," said Phoebe.

Anne frowned, perplexed. "But you did it."

"But I couldn't have if I had had time to think about it first. No, I couldn't. I am not brave. You know that. How often have you told me!"

"If I told you you weren't brave, I was wrong. To think I was the one who boasted that I could go off for a soldier. I couldn't have. I suppose you always knew I couldn't, didn't you?"

"No. I always thought you could do anything."

"And all the time it was you."

They stood together in the encroaching dark. It had begun to snow and the wind was sharper. The voices of people crossing the compound were so muffled that the two seemed to be completely alone. In a voice so low Phoebe had to strain to hear her, Anne said, "I'm sorry, Phoebe."

"It doesn't matter now," said Phoebe and knew that it didn't, that the hardness in her heart had softened.

"We'll be friends again, Phoebe, as we used to be."

"Yes," said Phoebe. But she didn't believe they would be, not as before. She and Anne were family. But friends? Had they ever really been friends? And now? So much had happened. So much had changed. She had changed. Anne had changed. She could not say all that to Anne, not now, when they were both still so hurt by each other and there was such sadness between them. All the same, when Anne asked, almost timidly, if she might walk to the commander's office with her, Phoebe said, "Of course," and waited for Anne to fetch her cloak. Then they walked, arms linked, in the silence of the snow.

By morning the wind had died, it had stopped snowing, and it was bright but bitterly cold. Phoebe stood outside the door of the barracks where she had been directed to settle herself with the Robinson family and the rest of the refugees. She had her hood up and her cloak pulled tightly around her, braving the cold to get away from the foetid air inside. She was wondering sadly if she would ever see her own beloved Connecticut River and her hills again. Would she be able to go home when the war was over? Would any of these refugees be able to go home? Would their homes be there for them?

Her melancholy thoughts were interrupted by the sound of crunching snow. She looked up to see Jem coming towards her from the river. He had his musket over his shoulder and a pack on his back.

"Phoebe," he said.

"Yes."

"Yes, well…" His voice trailed off.

Phoebe waited. And waited. "Yes, well, Jem?"

"Phoebe?" He was looking at her so intently

she began to feel uncomfortable. "Come walk with me down to the wharves." He took her hand and they walked. The only sound was that of their feet on the crisp white snow until they drew near the wharves, where men were busily chopping the ice from the bateau being readied for its journey up the St. Lawrence to Montreal.

"The last trip this winter, be my guess," said one of them cheerfully. Jem nodded.

"I'm goin' off on that boat," he said to Phoebe.

"I thought maybe that was it."

"I know all the things you're thinkin'. But I got to get into the war. I got to do my part."

"Isn't it enough you came all this way with your mother and Jeannie. Isn't it?" Phoebe looked at the stubborn set of his chin, the glint of determination that made the bright blue of his eyes almost green. There was nothing she could say to stop him. "Does your mother know?"

"Yes. Phoebe, will you miss me?"

She didn't want to answer that. She was afraid to miss Jem. She had lost too many people. She didn't want him to know that the memory of him standing in the dawn light on the mountainside telling her he cared about her had been the one thing that had kept her going all the way to the Richelieu River. But something in the way she looked at him must have told him.

"You will!" he cried, then in a much quieter voice, he said, "Phoebe, I'd ask you to marry me. Right now this minute I would, 'n' stay here with you — but, Phoebe, my country's in trouble 'n' you know I have to go."

Yes, she knew. Whatever made people want to go to war was powerfully strong. Hadn't she sent her father off to war? Hadn't she sent Gideon off to war? She shook her head angrily, shaking free the tears that had come to her eyes.

Jem put his musket on the ground. He took her by the shoulders. "We ain't married, Phoebe," he said, "but you got me t'keep whether you wants me or not, even if I ain't here. But when the war's over…Phoebe, when the war's over, if I come back all of a piece…Phoebe will you wait for me to see if I come back all of a piece?"

Phoebe stared at him. He was asking her to marry him.

"I don't guess I got the right to ask you to wait," Jem said, "but I'd sure admire for you to. It might not be so long. When General Howe and General Cornwallis gets goin' good 'n' proper they'll have them rebels licked in jig time. But I guess mebbe you don't… "

"Jem ——"

"You don't have to say," he interrupted quickly. "You can forget I asked. I got no business asking anyways, after you tramped halfway over the world on accounta that cousin you

249

cared so much for. I...well...Phoebe, I guess I'd take it kindly if I could go off with your blessin'."

"Jem ——"

"You shouldn't even have to ——"

"Jem, stop! Stop telling me what I shouldn't or don't have to do. You asked me something. Now I mean to answer you. Yes, Jem, I will send you away with my blessing. How could I do else? And Jem, yes, I will wait for you." She said this last so softly Jem had to ask her to say it again.

"Yes, Jem," Phoebe said loudly and clearly, "I will wait for you to come back from the war because...because I love you. I do, Jem. I do."

They stood there in the cold, clear morning light, looking at each other. Suddenly Jem looked like a stranger to Phoebe and, at the same time, he looked like the person she knew best in all the world. And she had told him she loved him.

The silence was broken by the shrill blast of the boat whistle.

"I got to go," said Jem. He pulled Phoebe to him and kissed her quickly and awkwardly on her mouth. "I love you, too," he whispered. He turned towards the boat. He turned back. They looked at each other, embarrassed. Then Phoebe put her hands up to his face, stood on tiptoe, and kissed him with all her heart. Then she put her arms around him and held him as though she would never let him go. Jem's arms went around her and they held each other until he broke free without a word. He picked up his musket and strode off to the boat.

Phoebe swallowed the lump in her throat. "God bless you and keep you, Jem Morrissay!" She called after him.

He raised his arm to let her know he had heard, but he did not look back. Phoebe knew he did not dare. She watched him board the ship and watched while he set his face to the west. She watched the soldiers in charge push off from the dock. She stood with the wind whipping her dark braid back and forth, the tears freezing on her face until the bateau had disappeared up the river.

Her journey was over. Gideon's message had reached the person to whom it was addressed. Even the coded message. Justus Sherwood had told her that it had to do with troop movements and rebel battle strategies, but he hadn't been free to tell her more. But he had stayed closeted with the General for hours the next day, and there was much coming and going of officers at the Sherwoods' house. A number of them stopped to praise her. She had done what she had set out to do, and the problems that had arisen from her impulsive act had been resolved. The past was the past. Whatever the future would bring she did not fear. She was no longer Anne's devoted young cousin, Gideon's little brown mouse, or Peter Sauk's little grey bird. She belonged to herself now. Phoebe Olcott, a complete person, and she was going to marry Jem Morrissay when he came back from the war.

Epilogue or how it all turned out

On a warm afternoon in early autumn in the year 1784, Phoebe Olcott sat spinning wool outside the door of Peggy and Charles Morrissay's log cabin on an island off the north shore of Lake Ontario. A large orange cat slept by her feet.

The American Revolution had been over for three years, although the treaty that officially ended the war had been signed only the year before. The British had lost, and the King's loyal American supporters had not been welcome back in their old homes. Their lands and possessions had been confiscated and their lives threatened.

And so the King had decreed that the Loyalists were to be given land in British North

America. Land was bought for them from the Micmac and Maliseet people in Nova Scotia, and from the Mississauga in Canada. The King's Mohawk allies who had lost their land in the Mohawk Valley in New York were given large tracts in Canada. Acres were parcelled out to every civilian Loyalist man according to the size of his family, and to every soldier according to his military rank plus the size of his family. Jem Morrissay's father, Charles, who had been a sergeant in the King's Royal Regiment of New York, was granted three hundred acres: two hundred for his rank, fifty for his wife, Peggy, and fifty for their daughter, Jeannie.

The new settlements began along the St. Lawrence River west of Montreal, branched up along the Ottawa, and west in the upper country along the north shore of Lake Ontario and its islands, all the way to the Niagara River. The Morrissays had taken their land on one of Lake Ontario's offshore islands, land that Justus Sherwood in his new job as Crown Surveyor had called "rich and good for meadow and pasture."

In the spring of 1784, after all those long years in the camps at Sorel and Yamachiche, the refugee Loyalists made their way by land as far as the rapids at Lachine, just west of Montreal, and, from there, by bateau to their new homes. Three thousand of them altogether, a flotilla of hopeful people, singing as they poled the low boats close to the shore.

Then, on a bright morning in May, when violets and trilliums filled the woods with colour, bluebirds and finches filled the air with song, and the scent of spring was everywhere, a collection of refugees stood on the rocky shore of Lake Ontario ready to pull their location tickets from the surveyor's hat. This had seemed to the Governor of Quebec the fairest way to distribute the land, to parcel it off into lots. Tickets with lot numbers on them were dropped into the hat. A man would step forward and pull a ticket from the hat to learn where his land would be. The Morrissays pulled their ticket and found themselves with their three hundred acres at the southeastern tip of the island, sixty safe miles across the lake from the country that had so recently been their own.

Among their neighbours were the people whom Peggy Morrissay had spent the war years with. Bertha Anderson, her son Johnny, and Betsy Parker were there. Bertha's husband, Septimus, had been killed fighting with Colonel Simcoe, but Johnny was now thirteen, old enough and strong enough to help chop down trees and build a cabin with his mother. Betsy was the same age, old enough and strong enough to do almost all the heavy work Johnny could do, as well as cook and spin and weave.

Lucy and Joseph Heaton, and Abigail Colliver, her husband, Jethro, who had miraculously survived months in the mine-shaft prison at Simsbury in Connecticut and another six years fighting with Butler's Rangers, their two children, Sam and Arnold, had land within ten miles along the shore from the Morrissays. Charity and Jonah Yardley (who still had George, now a fifteen-year-old cat) were only a few miles inland — old Aaron Yardley had died only the year before at Sorel. Margery and Thomas Bother and their five children were near neighbours. Their baby Zeke was now eight years old, and Tom, the infant born on the trail, was six. Peter Sauk and his family were to live on the Mohawk reserved lands only twenty-five miles away. Peter had come once to Fort Sorel to reassure himself that Phoebe had survived her journey, and again, at the end of the war, to tell her where he would settle.

The only family from those bad days in the wilderness journey that had not come to settle on the Lake Ontario island was the Robinson family. Only the year before, Anne had married a British soldier and gone to live in England. Five years earlier Aunt Rachael had been befriended by a French widow in Sorel Village and had decided to stay with Madame Boulanger. "The children," she had told Phoebe, "have come to feel at home here. They speak as much

French as English. I do not want to shift them again."

Phoebe hadn't liked leaving Aunt Rachael or the children, but it had been almost a relief to say goodbye to Anne. They had not been unkind to each other over the years in the refugee camp, but Phoebe had been wrong when she had thought Anne might have changed. Anne had remained as self-centred and full of romantic dreams as ever. Phoebe had felt sad to see her go off to London to a life that she knew was not going to be as grand as Anne envisioned. Billy Watson, the sergeant she had married, was a handsome man, but only a sergeant, not a man to provide the silks and satins and diamond buckles Anne still dreamed of. Phoebe had kept her reservations to herself, though. She had embraced her cousin and had seen her off with prayers and good wishes.

Phoebe had not wanted to stay in Sorel with Aunt Rachael. She had no desire to go home either, although she thought she would have been allowed because of her father having been a rebel. But she would not have felt at home in Hanover or in Orland Village anymore. Her friends were here in Canada. This was home now. So she had decided to go to Lake Ontario country with Jem's mother and father.

Jem had not come back from the war. His mother, his father, and Jeannie had all mourned for him. Friends had been sympathetic, but

Phoebe had not mourned. She had not believed he was dead. "He'll come, you will see," she had said confidently. "He asked me to wait for him. I'll wait."

People had whispered. She'd heard them. "Poor soul," they'd said, "she's like to be one of them that waits and waits all her life long, spinning and weaving for other folks' children." They'd shaken their heads sadly when Phoebe refused "that nice corporal Ben Larkin" who'd wanted to marry her, and despaired for her when she'd packed up her spare gown and shift, all she owned beside the one she wore (the deer-skin leggings and tunic had long since been worn to shreds and used to stuff chinks in the walls of the barracks). She had said her fare-wells to friends who had decided to stay on the Richelieu River or go away to the west, on the Niagara River. She had promised to send news often to Rachael and the children and gone to homestead with the Morrissays. She had taken with her the chest Rachael had brought from Orland Village, the one that had belonged to her grandmother. "You'll have something of us with you always," Aunt Rachael had said.

All this Phoebe was thinking about as she sat spinning in the warm sun that autumn after-noon, listening to the jays and crows, loving the spicy scent of wild rose-hips as it wafted towards her on every breeze.

"There," she said, "you are almost ready for the loom." She chuckled. "Phoebe Olcott, did you really think that hank of wool was set to tell you it was pleased? What are you coming to, talking to yourself like this? Are you...?" her voice trailed off. Her foot slowed on the treadle, her hand let go of the spindle. She had become aware that she was being watched.

She looked up to see a man standing at the edge of the clearing. He was a young man, hatless, his reddish-blond hair tied back, his red-bearded face so gaunt the bones would have been all you could see but for the blue of his eyes. He was dressed in fringed deerskin leggings and shirt, and he had a musket over one shoulder. He was leaning on a stick. He said nothing; he did not stir for what seemed a very long while. Then he raised an eyebrow and one corner of his mouth turned up.

Phoebe sighed. "Jem," she said.

"I'm all of a piece, Phoebe, exceptin' for a bit of a left-over limp. I was took prisoner. They only just let us free. Did you wait?"

"I have another cat. He's one of George's kittens. But no bear, Jem."

"Well, then, I reckon us three better find us a passel of land to build on." Jem moved from his spot by the trees.

Phoebe took a deep, shaky breath. She grinned at him. She put her foot back on the treadle, her hand on the spindle. "Now," she said, "you must wait for me — until I finish spinning this hank of wool for your mother."

Jem stepped back and propped himself against a tree. "I'll wait," he said.

Phoebe and Jem were married the next time the travelling preacher came their way. Jem was granted his soldier's land only a few miles from his mother's and father's, and there he and Phoebe cleared land and built their first log house. A few years later they sold it and bought land on a small bay at the west end of the island, land that Jem had discovered during a time he had gone with young Sam Colliver to help set up a mill on a nearby creek. Others besides Sam were setting up along that creek. Bertha Anderson's son John and his new wife, Lydia, Jonah Yardley, and young Tom Bother were among them.

"I'd like to call our bay Hawthorn Bay," Jem told Phoebe, "because it's ringed around with hawthorn trees 'n' my old gran told me once them trees mean good fortune."

Phoebe needed no persuading. From the moment she saw the bay glistening under a spring sun, and the little hawthorns covered with white blossoms, she had a deep sense of belonging.

"We will be well here," she said. "And our children and our children's children. We will all be well here. There will be peace in this country."

ALSO BY JANET LUNN

The Root Cellar

WINNER OF THE CLA CHILDREN'S
BOOK OF THE YEAR

It looked like an ordinary root cellar, the kind of place where you'd store canned goods, and winter vegetables. If twelve-year-old Rose hadn't been so unhappy in her new home, she probably never would have fled down the stairs to the dark cellar. And if she hadn't, she never would have climbed up into another century, the world of the 1860s, and the chaos of the American Civil War. There she makes her first friends—and they desperately need her help!

SEAL BOOKS / ISBN: 0-7704-2885-1

ALSO BY JANET LUNN

Shadow in Hawthorn Bay

WINNER OF THE CLA CHILDREN'S
BOOK OF THE YEAR
and
THE CANADIAN YOUNG ADULT BOOK AWARD

Born in the same week in the Highlands of Scotland, Mary Urquhart and her cousin Duncan had always been united by a wild joy for the land and for each other. Mary knows that Duncan's heart is always with her, even after he has left to seek his fortune in the raw wilderness of Upper Canada. Four years after he has left, Mary hears Duncan's cry for help across the great distance that separates them. Now, equipped with her strange gift of "second sight," Mary knows that she must leave behind all that is dear and safe and cross the ocean alone to find him.

SEAL BOOKS / ISBN: 0-7704-2886-X